TO ERIN,
THANK YOU FOR THE SUPPORT!
CHEERS!

Coming of RAGE

Short Fiction by
RAY VAN HORN, JR.

D1548344

Raw Earth Ink

2022

First paperback edition August 2022

ISBN 979-8-98504-069-2 (paperback)

Published by Raw Earth Ink
PO Box 39332
Ninilchik, AK 99639
www.taracaribou.com

For TJ,
You resurrected me and by doing so,
these stories have new life.

Also for my Boyo.
I understand far more than you'll ever know.

Table of Contents

Chasing the Moon

"SEND ME A POSTCARD from the revolution," I said to my reflection in the rearview mirror. It was only a Tuesday and the dreary puffballs beneath my eyes were cringe-worthy. The eyes themselves spoke of an afternoon spent looking down a highball glass in lament of the remaining slugs of bourbon I'd nursed since my layoff three months ago. Some people were functioning alcoholics. I was kinda-sorta functioning through sobriety. In a forced way, since I was already counting down to Christmas, and my Uncle Bob's dependable gift of a new fifth of Five Roses.

I busted my ass threading through a Baltimore beltway rush hour growing more ruthless by the month. 695 was always a crapshoot with more crap than shoot most weeknights. To stomach it on a routine basis, one needed the combination of a good salary, good tunes, and the constitution of good dodging skills. It was the only thing I didn't miss from being jobless.

I was giddier than a dance of depravity to slide past the customary highway crunch and down 83 South into Charm City with expedience. Whereas fifteen minutes was chewed up at home in verbal combat with my obdurate wife, Meghan, most of it had been made up on the drive with a hard thrum of Killing Joke spurring me on.

"Didn't get me today, buttheads," I told the traffic from behind my closed driver's side window.

My glory was a sham, considering the broil I carried with me on tonight's assignment. Meghan had given me a few choice words for having the wherewithal to cover another gig tonight instead of hammering out more resumes. Sure, I'd been laid off almost three months and our credit cards were near maxed. We'd eaten enough bungled hodgepodge meals from a dwindling pantry closet to the point takeout from Panera had become as extravagant as dining out at Carrabba's. Never underestimate a spouse's propensity to trash talk you behind your back as much as to your face when there's no room in the budget for sherry cordials and Ghirardelli chocolates.

I've spent more time job hunting each day than Meghan gives me credit for. I've been so gelded by her these days I couldn't come up with a good finish to our brutal parting exchange:

"Twenty-seven years I've given to a man child," she'd said with one of those obnoxious sighs I could honestly push her down a jagged cliff over. "A jobless one, at that."

"Maybe you might consider asking yours for more hours," I countered. "It'd be a refreshing change of pace, not having to hold the bag by myself after all these years."

"Oh, boo hoo, Mick. Do you see this?"

You've no doubt seen it before; everyone has. The snide, near pinching of a thumb and forefinger gliding back and forth in opposite directions with a smidge of space between them.

"Here we go again," I fired back with only half of my verbal cannonade. The cannon itself had been locked in some forgotten armory near an untested battlefield. "The world's smallest violin playing 'My heart bleeds for you.'"

"Right you are," Meghan told me, chopping the air between us with an extended forefinger.

"Get some new shtick," I groused at her.

"Get a clue, rock fogy," she retaliated, unperturbed by my insurrection. "A job would be better."

I've had to first show her my job contact log before submitting it to the unemployment office for my weekly checks, lest my ears be filled with nagging over how desperate things were getting. It came always after Meghan's two o'clock nap, when most personnel managers are finishing lunch, by her estimation. In my old business, the personnel managers eat in-between compliance calls and they're tougher to get on the horn than Mike Patton of Faith No More.

Meghan had already grown impossible long before my layoff and I was on the verge of filling out a Mickey Dee's app, just to get away from her mouth. I'd already come to praise *The Young and the Restless* and *Judge Judy* for taking her away from the second of two swivel chairs in our shared office. If I had to hear one more time how much my ex-boss, Frank Stanton, was the reason she couldn't order more printer ink and I was no better for being at home instead of an office, I was going to smash her chair down to its rollers. Just because.

The real estate market was drier than a desert town at summer's peak and my two-weeks unpaid cell phone had only rung once with a gruff-voiced president of a Mom-and-Pop title company on the other end, Tom Pinder. The conversation didn't get beyond hello and my answer to Tom's blunt query for my salary requirements. Even lowballing myself didn't get me the job.

To quote Meghan this evening before I whumped the townhouse door behind me, I was an unworthy slackass, even though my concert coverage tonight was for pay. Of course, the $150.00 I'd have transmitted online through PayPal would cover my gas and food outlay and maybe part of the cell phone bill, which was Meghan's point. My point of cutting off her tablet and fewer Kindle downloads in the interim went into an invisible rejection pile she kept for most of my domestic proposals.

Regardless of my angst which would've served my long-forgotten 17-year-old self better than it does three decades later, I got to The Kat's Kradle on Howard Street with five minutes to spare coming into the 6:00 hour. I may have won favor from the commuting gods, but, go figure, the conciliation meant my on-site interview was delayed. As if I should be surprised, much less maintain the same level of professionalism with a young psychobilly band dubbed The Hearse Hoppers as I would behind the desk at a Fortune 500 brokerage.

Why I bothered covering gigs anymore was attributed to a mulish refusal to give up this part of my problematical life. A cantankerous spouse, a mouthy, pregnant teen and being downsized from a less-than-Fortune 500 mortgage title company represented the top layer of my issues.

Beneath those laid looming foreclosure, lost health benefits, creditors hounding us for non-payment and the manifestation of an ex-girlfriend, Destiny, whose dorm room at Towson University and the back seat of her old Geo Prism were our natural habitat in easier days. They used to call it Towson State University then, or Towson State, to the alumni of the day. Nowadays, the state funding has become *non esset*. It looked like I wasn't the only one taking a chomp from a shit pie these days.

Destiny had fallen on some hard times herself these days, so she'd said after tracking me down through Facebook a month ago. Her finances were nowhere near as kaput as mine since she'd made a name for herself in a downtown marketing firm as its veep of operations. She drives a 2021 red Tesla Model 3 these days, so it's hard to muster any fiscal sympathy. Still, she was miserable as crud. She had a cheating husband and two half-wit sisters she was half supporting, all bleeding her tolerance. She'd been adamant about having no kids and it was far too late to start now. Destiny had sent me an emoji with a blank expression when I offered her my teenage two-for-one package in jest. As if to tell me, like Meghan had less than an hour ago, to get real.

Destiny had been married eleven years and taken her sweet time settling down. I was jealous of that, to be honest. It was like time had only aged *us*, not our ability to fall into a quick, candid rhythm with each other. After spilling my guts about my problems at home, Destiny had sent me an hour's worth of electronic catch ups.

She told me she'd jumped the fence for a month with a handful of chicks at her gym while her husband, Brock (a fartknock name for a supreme fartknocker), was doing everybody but her. Ultimately, she'd decided the hopeless lesbian act was just that. Swearing me to secrecy through the confidence of an instant message, she told me she was man-hunting again on the sly. This after contracting a yeast infection once Brock had smoke screened his husbandly duties by taking her from behind half asleep in the middle of the night.

Destiny's profile pic was scorching at 49, but I could see the same shatter inside her eyes I did in mine on the drive into the city. Instant Message and an instant frenzy to regain a part of me that had been lost at home, in the workplace, even on assignments that were growing harder to secure, compelled me to drop Destiny my digits.

She'd told me she still rocked a thong without my asking and the snap she'd texted me earlier in the week backed her claim, cutesy dimples and all. Nobody in our age bracket had business looking so good, though she confessed having to dye her hair once a month to retain a softer shade of her original chestnut locks. If I hadn't known Destiny's body so intimately, even the scar trailing from her left shoulder down to her southpaw waist (gained in her teens from a swimming accident), I would've sworn the pic had been Photoshopped. She'd pitched softball in college as a leftie, everything that involved me back then from the right.

We'd had a grand ol' time in our college years and thinking about those days of naked liberty had injected a poisonous detestation toward my mouthy, contrary wife and our ungrateful, freeloading daughter. The more I let the tumbling anger fester inside of me, the brighter a candle I'd relit since Destiny had reached out.

The neighborhood surrounding The Kat's Kradle was a befuddled culture clash of urban toughs and wayfaring art students from the nearby Maryland Institute of College Arts—or MICA, as the local literati called it. They uttered it like the name of an elite sanction, as the area music heads who studied at The Peabody Conservatory downtown called it (and themselves by self-ordained omnipresence) "Peabody."

"Lamar Jackson or Patrick Mahomes?" I heard from a tall, lanky guy wearing a purple Baltimore Ravens sweatshirt which ran down both rails of his wiry hips.

"C'mon, bruh," his half-sized companion clad in a faded Eminem shirt and tugging on a lit doob replied. Whatever he had rolled up, it had him staggering about, banging into his taller friend. "The fugg you doin' gettin' all up in my business?"

"Asking you a question about football, dick licker. You're stoned as fuck, man."

Another guy passed me in the parking lot, a Caucasian guy with coffee colored whitey dreads bopping his bony ass as he dropped some terrible, clichéd rap going along the lines of "I'm an arsonist who burns with a pen, meditation, contemplation, just call it Zen...I dual-wield this shit, my words are dope, you don't agree, I'll shank you, hang you from a rope..."

None of them going anywhere near my direction toward rock music.

That colorful dynamic to be counted, this was as depressed-eclectic an area in north-central Baltimore as it came. Hanging out in the streets where The Kat's Kradle was located treated you to a mouth-watering array of Italian, Moroccan, Thai and Korean grub. Half of the people in the district looked haggard or bored. Others like they spent all night binging Netflix on a caffeine bomb with a hit of crystal meth.

The rats had no problem making themselves known as did the area pickpockets, gangbangers and pimp wannabes. There was only one gas station within blocks, and it had a history of stickups dating back to the Seventies. Stubborn as the residents who took the shit with their sugar, and neither were going anywhere.

I'd be passing on the overpriced venue beers and band merch Meghan had been chiding me for well before things turned hardnosed between us. She did have a point, given my home office closet was stuffed with three decades' worth of band tees, including a few outgrown Queensryche, Sepultura and Bad Brains relics I've refused to part with.

I, of course, was expected to understand Meghan's need for lottery tickets, Coach Purse knockoffs, manicures, and Sudoku puzzle books. Since being put on the bread line, all these went away, save for the lottery tickets. Meghan works 25 hours a week at home as a customer service rep for the Carroll County Department of Taxation. I hear, no less than four times a week, how our fortunes will change once she hits the Mega Million. The biggest payout she's ever nabbed was twenty bucks from a state lottery scratch off.

Upon my arrival to the club, I'd called to check in with the Hearse Hoppers' hoodwink tour manager who went by the goofball handle, "Sneed." Sneed's embryonic voice differentiated from his band's juvie demographic only in the minute way a 19-year-old bass player did from his twenty-something bandmates. He told me the Hearse Hoppers were having dinner in another part of town. As luck would have it, they'd left fifteen minutes prior to my arrival at the venue. Karma, I guess, for revisiting old times and positions tried with Destiny, but not Meghan, inside my head while racing a troublemaking soccer mom in her Dodge Caravan down the offramp between 795 and 695.

Since the Hearse Hoppers weren't on the premises yet, I slipped back into my Ranger pickup in a compact area comprising the parking lot behind The Kat's Kradle. This aggravating wait was a real pisser, since there'd been no established interview time, only the instructions from the band's publicist to call upon arrival to the venue.

At least I got to avoid listening to Meghan needle how she was just skimming above minimum wage, while Cait sat on our couch or in her bedroom sulking and pissing about her life being over now that she was with child.

I was chasing after bands half my age with a digital hand recorder, pretending I still had "the life." Most rock journalists today Skype from home, yet I feel more at home and engaged with a band on-site. My interviews lick with insider's chops, having been a short-time six string road warrior in another life. I have the pictures of me yowling overtop the same Gibson Sunburst I pawned for six hundred bucks a week ago. Broke my heart more than Meaghan saying to me in dismissal instead of thanks: "Good. It's been taking up space in the closet for too long."

The lingo I know is nothing you see on behind-the-scenes music specials nor in the half-assed Q&A sessions fielded in the B-level mags and amateur blogs beginning with the hackneyed query, *"Who are your influences?"* and queef with *"Do you have anything else you'd like to tell our readers?"* I have in my arsenal corpulent craftsman phrases such as "frammis," "flip-coil" and "down rigger." Of course, those are often edited out of the article's final print since the average reader is interested more in the stimuli instead of the technical portions of music making. Algorithms also say the average time today's reader spends reading a piece online instead of a hard copy magazine is 55 seconds to the former's eight to ten minutes.

Meghan's harping condemnations be damned, she's right to say I'm out of place. Eighteen years covering underground music, I keep rolling toxic encouragement in the back of my head the editors at *Rolling Stone* will see my eventual Hearse Hoppers article and live photos then offer me an assignment. I'll ace that one and *Village Voice* would be next. Up the ladder I'd go, one delusional rung at a time. I've carried the same dream forever, taking it on a road to nowhere, though I feel confident I'll one day spot David Byrne waving at me from the shoulder of a rock 'n roll Route 66.

With nothing to do in wait other than fiddling inside my pocket thinking about Destiny, I switch the vibe in my truck to Joy Division, feeling much of the fuck-the-world blues prompting Ian Curtis to check out to the tune of an atrocity exhibition.

It appeared I was getting the interview *after* the gig, which meant a long, dumb wait for the band to schmooze with their fans and sell enough t-shirts, ball caps and albums—survival money into the next city. I'd been there. I knew how it all worked. At least the venue bouncers knew me and wouldn't chase me off the premises as they would everybody else by show's end. A lot of favorable press and tips to the right bartenders kept my good standing. Alas for them, I'd be taking a free ride this evening, right down to the guest list entry and miserable pours out of the complimentary water cooler.

This being a psychobilly show—think Brian Setzer with a sped-up mean streak and a penchant for horror flicks—the kids blundering into The Kat's Kradle were all decked out for a mutant sock hop.

Across-the-board, the girls sported precarious Bettie Page sculpts. The guys were what I called "whiffleheads," dudes bearing Fifties retro leveled flattops, some as high as six inches off their scalps. Others gelled their long strands into towering liberty spikes, a preening descendent of the UK82 mohawk made fashionable by The Exploited, GBH and their Ois-in-passing. There was one femmehawk to be counted, hers being dyed pink and indigo for extra credit.

The would-be sick girls were mashes of poodle skirt priss and roughneck sleaze offset by their fishnet leggings and combat boots. A lot them were punctured with silver nose and lip rings. Their male counterparts wore nad-smashing jeans and black or white t-shirts, some plastered with band names like The Chop Tops, Nekromantix, and Tiger Army, but mostly they wore basic Fruit of the Loom or Hanes undershirts. Many wore the same Ali Boulala brothel creeper loafer (hijacked from the skater scene), as if a fire sale on them had transpired somewhere in Baltimore's version of Kings Road. Some clomped around in winklepicker replicas. As if to mimic their greaser grandfathers, some of the drape replicates rolled cigarette packs up their right sleeves so they rested smack atop their knobby shoulders. Considering you couldn't smoke in the bars now, it was as much a show as the rest of their on-loan ensemble.

Both the boys and gals bore arm-length sleeve tattoo patterns, which they ogled upon one another and shared stories about the people they'd inked with—and in a few cases, slept with. Tit for tat, as it were. I counted four skin renditions of Glenn Danzig in passing, plus one Johnny Cash. A lot of the guys had cheap fabric key straps hanging out of their pockets in DIY fashion, while the truly hardcore sung bruising pain from their hip-flogging chain wallets. One meaty kid had on a dusty leather jacket with a tattered Subhumans patch safety-pinned to the back. No doubt his dad's at one time. Ditto for the squirmy, skinny girl with a long brown ponytail standing by her lonesome; she was wearing a vintage, faded Nuclear Assault shirt. Hell, that one might've been mine when it was still new.

The whole parade was borrowed from a multitude of eras past, and I found it all gaudy. Of course, this comes from someone wearing economical no-name sneakers, jeans from the doorbuster rack and a faded Police t-shirt with the album cover for *Regatta de Blanc* I've had since 1983. Astonishing enough, it still fit years later. The sad news, it didn't quite reach my crotch. If I could send myself a message in a bottle to that kid back then, I might tell him to go large instead of medium.

Only my left hoop earring (punctured back in this morning after these long, fruitless weeks of no gainful means) gave me street cred amidst these kids, although I stood out like a party-crashing schoolteacher. You should've seen my feathery, dirty-blond locks back in the day. I looked like the younger Stewart Copeland on my chest. After Destiny tracked me down, she joked how she'd humped me so much back then because I'd looked like Sebastian Bach with a hair trim. I gave her my number for that roundabout compliment, knowing it was not only ballsy, but it was also the opening to a door I had no business unlocking.

Buzzkill, how does it happen when your scene no longer belongs to you? What defined you at a youthful age gets killed off then comes back two decades later when you can tell the greenhorns all they've missed. Unless you're onstage where senior bands (now called "heritage acts") receive their due for a second go-round, you no longer matter. You're the weirdo, the assclown, even more so than when you practiced it all first.

In my case, I'd been on the stage a lifetime ago, not that it mattered to this generation, much less my own. Even Caitlin could care less and she digs all of those proto-pop metal revival acts like Skillet, Lacuna Coil and Evanescence. We never have seen eye-to-eye much, but my baby girl having a baby of her own without forcing the soon-to-be-deadbeat father into stepping up to his obligations, you can imagine how I took her saying I'm a loser for not having a new job yet.

By the time I checked back with Sneed, I was told the Hearse Hoppers were on their way back but wouldn't be ready for the interview until after the gig. Slamdango, I knew how to call it. I prayed Meghan would take a Unisom before I came home—half the bottle if our marriage meant anything to her.

Sneed said we could probably do a quick ten-minute interview after their set at the band's van while they loaded their gear up—apropos when you have no real job. Of course, I didn't have one either, so who was I to judge?

I got back out of my truck as the club was about to open and the Betties and Whiffleheads were lined up with their driver's licenses and photo ID's (some as bogus as an AMA acceptance speech) already clutched in their hands. The line wrapped in an L shape from the sheer metal door of the front entrance, reminiscent of those daunting iron barricades in the *Get Smart* credits. I laughed to myself, thinking these kids wouldn't know Don Adams from John Adams—though *Sam* Adams was no doubt a part of their vernacular.

The queue ended near the army green dumpster which carved a huge slice out of the miniscule parking lot. In the past I'd seen a lumpy rat the size of a 14 athletic shoe and a whitish spot atop its left shoulder leap out of that dumpster and scare the raunchy business out of people, myself included. After covering so many gigs at The Kat's Kradle and seeing that plump ol' rodent show up almost every time, I'd given it a name: Atlas.

A local punk band called Dirty Trace was the opener tonight and due on by 7:45. Normal protocol was the club stalled the show a full hour from doors open to rake in their first couple tills of drink profits from those who could imbibe. Plus, it was considered social hour where regional musicians congregated over pints and shots to keep one another abreast of their latest projects and who they knew in the industry. Having listened to them from afar and sometimes in their direct company, most of it was a dick pull.

I began scratching gibberish in the pocket notepad I used to jot my questions whenever I did on-location interviews. I had my usual twelve questions for the Hearse Hoppers, but I saw myself narrowing it down to the six or seven best, given the slimming margin of time I was going to get with them.

I began to describe the alley next to The Kat's Kradle where the bands always parked. I jotted anecdotes for future writings about the broken glass, saturated gig schedules, and ripped open condom wrappers. I tried to look the part of a serious rock journalist while hovering near the vans, all of which (even Dirty Trace's with the fewest logged road miles of the three) were the identical gray metal sausages my thrash metal band, Death Splinters, had run around back in 1989. Not exactly the glory days Springsteen warns to never you let pass by; we'd failed to heed his advice once Death Splinters broke up a year after its formation. Our doofy band name should be a good clue as to why.

Finally, the club opened and a unified cheer sounding more like a cynical doom fugue instead of a more apropos rebel yell went up from the front of the line to the back in a weird, echoing wave.

Most of the adolescent quiffs, crew cuts and devilocks were branded at the door with a magic marker "X" on their left hands, designating they were underage. At one point in fringe rock history that "X" was a sign of straight edge punk, which meant those bearing the brand lived by clean principles: no drinking, no smoking, no snorting, no fucking, and no discrimination. Straight edge was making a comeback, albeit with a heavier, militant message to include no meat consumption, self-empowerment, and join-us-or-spit-out-your-teeth statutes.

A flock of Betties honked through the alley, glancing over at the vans curiously and then at me. One of them, who wore horn-rimmed glasses (geek chic, to my generation) whistled at me, grabbed her plump tits which were pushing out of her peeled, blood red button-down, jiggled them up and down and then dragged her moist jailbait tongue along her maroon-tinted upper lip, leaving a glistening veneer. She also wore one of those prosaic Catholic school skirts around her snap case hips I would've thought delicious and sinful if she hadn't been San Quentin quail. Her Betties-in-arms squawked behind her and they muttered in perfect synchro "He wishes," before they slithered to the band vans and peeked into the windows.

I forced away an awful picture of my daughter, about the same age of this bespectacled Bettie, the latter flaunting her goodies at potential rapists just to impress her in-a-hurry-to-grow-up friends. Caitlin had flaunted her assets at some teen coward shagmaster named Kevyn, whose coward family refused our calls and then moved their irresponsible progeny to another state after he'd knocked Cait up. A confrontation was due, but Caitlin wasn't even interested in throwing down.

My pocket buzzed and I thumbed my cell phone off its lock while fishing it out. Destiny had sent me a text message.

"Where u at right now, Mick? At a show, right? I'm in a mood to chase the moon. I'll pick you up if you want a better offer than that subcultural mess of a night out. I'll even treat you to some crab cake subs first if you want to ditch that poor boy scene a few hours and revisit some old memories. They don't deserve us, just saying."

I don't know what I sound like gasping since I'm almost always too shocked and too in the moment whenever I do. This time, I heard myself and it sounded like I used to back in the day with Destiny. Chasing the moon, we'd called it, driving off to nowhere after grabbing a bite and then each other. Always at night. We'd take turns driving, but the destination always came quicker with her behind the wheel.

I hated my wife, sure, but could I go through with this? It wasn't so much the fact Meghan had held off from me for seven months, and then it was a quiet, lay-down-and-take-it birthday gift I could've given myself with more passion. The temptation to take Destiny up on her offer was spiked by Meghan's lack of passion, *period,* except to give me shit at 8:30 in the morning before I start hunting for job contacts. These days, it's not as simple as cracking open a newspaper on Sundays and combing five or six pages of want ads. These days, there are no printed want ads at all, much less readers of newspapers.

Before I could come up with a response which would sentence me to

Satan's perpetual waiting room, my cell rang. It was Sneed.

"Yo, boss man, sorry to do this to you, but the guys got hung up somewhere in what you guys call 'Little Italy' around here. Anyway, I was just informed we're bolting out of town first thing to catch a new date in Yonkers we were just confirmed for. Gonna need to re-book this for another time. Hope you understand. You're still on the list for the show with photo, though. Do you mind emailing what you get to the band's website?"

I wanted to rip into Sneed, informing him I'd busted my ass getting down here for the interview, and this was substandard treatment. I knew better, though. I'd also been through it many times before. Things like this were as commonplace in music promotion as publicists using over-embellished laurels as "black metal alchemists" or "proto-math metal heroes" in their press releases. Hype men and women who wish they were writing comic books.

I held my tongue because you never know when you could be blackballed for sniping at someone in the industry. People seem like they're tender vittles one day, but many have a surprising way of surging into power positions later.

"Alright, man," I said, leaving Sneed a sigh to chew on. "I'll call Jenn at Strike Force and reschedule."

"You're the shit, dude!" Sneed exclaimed on his end. "Enjoy the show."

Click and silence, save for the chatter amidst the Whiffleheads and Betties in line.

Right then, I became disinterested in elbowing my way to the stage amongst a bunch of teenaged hicks 'n tricks who would just as soon see me hit the bricks. The Kat's Kradle never afforded a barrier between the stage and the crowd for their bouncers and press. It was always a guaranteed free-for-all. At a psychobilly show, it would be a guaranteed keep-your-ass-up-before-you-get-stomped-on-for-all.

I'd interviewed the godfather of the psychobilly freakout, Reverend Horton Heat. I'd even interviewed the Twang Thang himself, Duane Eddy, who, along with Link Wray, Eddie Cochran, the Misfits and The Cramps invented this chili-con-carnage. And I was wasting my time on these low tier cowpunks? Yippee-ki-yi-fuck-you.

Atlas made his usual appearance as I headed back to my Ranger, sending a fresh arriving pack of Betties into a screaming tizzy. The boys trailing behind them laughed and threw rocks at the fat rodent, who outmaneuvered each lob. I swear Atlas wiggled his nose twice in defiance at those boys. It wasn't just teenage humans who sought rebellion.

I pulled up Destiny's text message again and read it three times. My hands shook and I almost dropped the phone.

I looked up into the darkening sky to detect the moon, only a quarter full, a waxing crescent. It represented the Mother Goddess—Isis, told to me by my late grandmother a pocketful of summers ago—in her infancy stage. A symbol of hope, renewal and optimism. A fresh start.

After I was alone in the parking lot again, Atlas peered at me, frozen in place. From where I was, the rot of spoiled vegetables and discarded diapers chuffing from the dumpster made me wonder how rats had the stomach for refuse.

"Should I do it?" I asked Atlas, not even caring if I was heard, much less seen doing something so absurd. Worse, I waggled my cell phone in my palm at the hairy gnawer, as if the gesticulation transcended the communication gap between species.

I'd swear on the life of my future grandchild Atlas jerked his head toward the right, then the left before scampering off. His thick, pink tail flapped at me faster than a hurricane warning flag. He'd given me his answer.

"Godspeed, rat," I said with a smirk and nodded, the same as I did in appreciation of a straggling teenager wearing nothing more ostentatious to a Hearse Hoppers show than I did. Without mouthing it aloud, I congratulated the kid's audacity to sport jazz maestro, Miles Davis across his chest. That was retro done right.

Swiping my cell back on after it winked out, I took another gander into the sky, thinking of Grandma and wondering what a woman with wings who kissed her children worldwide with moonbeams in her eyes might truly look like. Assuming Isis was real, perhaps she was blessing me right now with a promise of a better future. It felt every much the test I knew it was. Hell, it had been a test ever since seeing Destiny's barely aged, pocked behind come across my phone.

I began to compose a response to Destiny that began with *"Maybe they don't…"* until I sighed in mid-thought.

The rest would stay locked inside my head after I hit delete to the whole thing.

Watching Me Fall

THE TEARS HAD COME again.

So had the cramps in her abdomen.

The pale walls around Allison seemed more stark than usual, the glaring white upon her untanned skin like a spotlight with the intent of whittling gone her remaining sliver of control. Her urine was gridlocked and the more Allison struggled to push it out, the sicker she felt.

As the bathroom sink next to her went *whoosssshhh* over and over, it felt like her ordinarily quiet little world was about to implode. The incremental spritzes of water and the subsequent gurgles down the drain were not just annoying the shit out of Allison, it presented to her a sound of finality, of being trapped. Worse, of being held hostage. She knew that feeling all too well.

"I don't know how you do it, girl," her best friend, Leah, said, toweling off her dripping face. "I can't go to the bathroom with anyone near me."

"That makes two of us," Allison said in a low growl, hoping Leah would get the message. She'd been grateful for the company last night, even more so after seeing the news flash across the header of her phone at work yesterday. It had been an update she'd never expected to see, at least not for many more years. She'd unsubscribed from HotMinuteNews.net right away in response.

Allison twirled the empty spindle of the toilet paper holder as her left leg lulled and tingled, growing numb from her prolonged sit on the toilet. The cold, metal cylinder spool seemed to mock her. Allison was waiting for Leah to get done and get gone, lest she expose herself to get up and fetch a new roll. The longer Leah kept at it, nattering about the episodes of *Euphoria* they'd binged on HBO Max the prior night, the more aggravated Allison was getting. She only remembered Zendaya and Hunter Schaefer were in the cast. Zendaya had been trapped in a smoky haze of her own making in the beginning of the series. Beyond that, Allison had her mind blasted far from the steamy shenanigans going on which had Leah gabbing like the bathroom sink was a workplace water cooler.

Right now, a stupid unfilled toilet spindle was the least of Allison's problems. Anything threatening to come bursting out of her seemed intent on staying there. Just to make her mood worse. The sourness in her belly had nothing to do with the takeout beef lo mein and shrimp toast she'd forced herself to eat last night. Nor were the two bottles of Corona to blame. She hadn't wanted any of it, but Leah had insisted on a girls' overnight "done right."

Leah's forwardness right now was unexpected and the longer she babbled on, she was growing even more clueless to Allison's plight.

As a child, Allison's mother used to hover and coax Allison to speed up her business whenever she was taking too long on the potty. It had been hard to think of it anything but a control thing. Thus, Allison had grown up and grown uncomfortable with the prospect of another human being occupying her space when she needed to go. Forget public bathrooms. Allison used them in extreme emergencies only and often she'd hold her business if it didn't mean soiling herself.

Leah's thin brown bob cut just below her ears screeched of bed head. She'd done a poor job rinsing off her makeup last night before they'd turned in, and now watching Leah groan and paw at her smeared face with the sink water gushing into her fingers gave Allison an unexpected smile.

"What'd we eat last night, again?" Leah asked as she pushed her face within inches of the vanity mirror. It appeared Leah hadn't been too fond of what she was seeing in the reflection, judging by the flickered sneer and a bemoaned rolling up of her eyes. To Allison, Leah reminded her of herself many years ago, nudging her then-chubbier face before a mirror to pop pimples in a tizzy or to hunt for wrinkles her mother threatened would come earlier than expected if she didn't lose enough weight. She loved her mother and she missed her mother. She didn't miss her mother's confounded vexing.

"Lo Mein," Allison grunted. "No offense, Leah. I'm not feeling myself and I'm stuck here without a roll of tp. Do you mind?"

The pain in her stomach was driving her nuts almost as much as her own pestering voice which had nothing good to say right now. It wheedled on Allison to kick Leah out so she could finally pee.

"Oh, snap, I'm sorry, girl," Leah said. "Where do you keep your rolls? I'll get one for you."

"Hallway closet, upper shelf. You can't miss them."

A moment of silence, then Allison heard Leah call out, "Damn, Ally, you're not kidding. Forty-eight rolls worth? You still worried about COVID shortages?"

"Did you go a full week without any toilet paper?" Allison answered in a sarcastic tone. "I had to pinch some from my job by stuffing long wads into my pockets until the stores had some again. That was a real low."

"Here you go, sweetie," Leah said, returning to Allison with her back turned and a full roll extended out. "I'll give you some privacy. I hope you keep coffee around here and I hope even more it's not decaf."

"Thanks. Yes, I have a Keurig and take your pick between Mountain Roast and Hazelnut."

"My hero," Leah said, leaving the bathroom and closing the door for Allison.

Allison had grown used to living alone; this considering her bachelorette's pad was hardly a typical apartment. To the north within two hundred meters to remind her, was the old Tudor house and its likewise solitary owner, Mr. Croker.

Allison's place had once been a servant's quarters for a mansion which had burned down in the late 1800's, long after Sherman and his Yankee troops had torched and looted the same Georgian tobacco-producing grounds during the Civil War. The surviving plantation cabin had reportedly stashed up to thirteen slaves up through the age of Antebellum, many of whom stayed on after Emancipation because there'd been nowhere else to go amidst Sherman's rampages.

After the Tudor went up by Mr. Croker's father, a local textiles merchant who'd invested most of his humble fortune into his rebirthed manor, the offshoot dwelling had been refurbished into a guest house. After Mr. Croker inherited the entire estate following his father's death in 1967, the guest house became an efficiency apartment. Allison became its nineteenth tenant, as conveyed to her by Mr. Croker's caregiver (and official business handler), a plump but powerfully built woman she knew only as "Dru." Allison's place was modular in shape instead of the standard rectangular divisions you found in the standard apartment complexes. No corridors here, just a sprawled kitchen-dining room-living room combo with a bed and bath carved into the rear of the place. Perfect for a single tenant, just comfy enough for two, so long as the second person wasn't a permanent occupant. Allison often wondered how 13 people once managed to live in this former cabin at the same time.

The only drawback to living here was Allison couldn't breathe every time she went up to the Tudor to hand over her rent check. Its archaic stuffiness and the pervading choke of both pipe and cigarette tobacco was enough to squash her lungs. That was only a few minutes or so of suffocation as Dru waved Allison inside, took the check from her and handed her a written receipt, always with the salutation, "Mr. Croker appreciates your prompt payment." Allison wondered if Dru had lungs of steel living inside the manor, since she'd never seen the estate manager smoke.

Hers was a cramped little place, but nowhere near as cramped as Allison's insides, which hollered at her the longer it took to urinate. A few dribbles had come, but not the merciful stream she was desperate for.

It was the first time since Allison had moved here she'd had an overnight guest.

She'd first met Leah in their college years at Kennesaw State University and the friendship had stuck these five years after both graduated Summa Cum Laude, Allison with a degree in Early Childhood Education, Leah in Informational Technology. They'd both found jobs fast, which sometimes presented the girls with scheduling conflicts when they wanted to get together. Leah's job in IT for a local trading brokerage had her working traditional 9:00 to 5:00 days maybe twice a week. She was often held late and sometimes worked on the company servers remotely from home, as late as until one in the morning.

With both of her parents gone to the next life and Leah her only friend outside of Brighter Horizons Day Care where she worked at, isolation was what Allison had sought out.

Allison's privacy had been of the utmost importance to her, no doubt the reason Dru leased the place out to her on Mr. Croker's behalf. Allison didn't cause waves and she was only seen by the lights inside the house. Since she'd moved here, Allison came and went to work, nestling on the sofa on evenings she wasn't hanging with Leah. She entertained herself with either the television or a book and that suited her just fine most nights. Most of the time, it was a conventional and blessedly boring microcosm.

Until yesterday.

Shocking enough when the news came across her cell. It was later all over the news, even CNN and Fox. It was on all the music channels, reporting his release like sports stations reported team releases of controversial athletes who beat up their children and significant others. Bird-in-hand, Allison called it.

Allison never said anything to Leah. Yet the headline badgered Allison all night and into the bleak, sleepless hours of the morning. She'd slept maybe a couple of hours in and out while Leah snuffled next to her, sounding worse than the truism about snores and buzzsaws.

He was free again.

Seven years ago, she'd prayed for his incarceration and rejoiced when she'd been answered. Allison had watched the near-daily reports of The Brigadiers' drummer Jake McCray's trial back then, angry with herself for never coming forward to ice the deal. It would have been worth the near five hours' flight from Atlanta to Los Angeles, just to make sure the jury made the right call.

A year after what McCray had done to Allison, he'd gone away for an entirely different set of charges—drug distribution and second-degree assault. The latter, he'd been given the full judgment of seven years, slapped with another ten for peddling cocaine to other Los Angeles musicians and high-profile clientele in the city government. Of all things, considering what the cruel son of a bitch was capable of. Celebrities seldom paid their due penalties in full for criminal behavior, as far as Allison was concerned. Not to the same measures as ordinary criminals. To Allison, a criminal was a criminal, and no matter if this one was the drummer in a famous rock band, Jake McCray should never have been set free so early from prison.

When he'd been sentenced, Allison started breathing easier, no longer fearing oblong shadows with the suspicion he was creeping up on her. Always she looked over her shoulders, checking to see if McCray was there like he'd once been, eight years ago. Never there but always a threat to reappear.

Yet he was free again. *Free.* Any assumptions justice had been served died inside of Allison along with the embryo she'd nearly come up with a male and female name for. That was until she'd decided she didn't want to see *his* face ever again. She loved children so much she'd chosen a career in the industry. Yet having one carrying the DNA of Jake McCray, Allison couldn't *not* abort it, much as she'd cried for days at herself after the fateful day at Grasonville Planned Parenthood. It had only taken a pill, but it was as heartbreaking to Allison as if she'd terminated the fetus in-clinic 21 weeks after missing her period.

Free.

Leah hadn't yet arrived last night to see Allison sink to her knees, shivering and weeping, feeling encapsulated, like it was all happening all over again. The twinges in Allison's privates became fresh again, along with a startling ache in her guts. Amidst her shock and grief after the announcement McCray was out on early parole, Allison was unaware she'd pushed her bottom into the air as she grabbed herself around the waist and bawled into the carpet. The staggering realization hit her a few moments later, and it sent her sprinting for her bed to scream into her pillows. No sign Dru had heard anything, thank God.

"You okay in there, Ally?" Leah chimed from outside the bathroom. "I gotta leave for work. I'm borrowing your Sailor Moon travel mug for the coffee, okay? I'll bring it back next time."

"K," Allison said back, forcing all the anguish from her voice before a new batch of tears slid down her face.

"Catch you later, girl. The overnight was a cool idea. Want to do it again tonight? I'm already hooked on *Euphoria* and can't wait to see episode six. I can bring grub again. I'm feeling Mediterranean."

"Yeah, sure," Allison murmured, though she felt elated inside to know she would have Leah around for whatever came next.

Leah at least knew what had happened to Allison all those years ago. Not much of a newsperson, though, it was evident Leah had no clue Jake McCray had been sprung from prison. All her time spent around computers and web browsers, Leah was ironically the least informed person in all of Georgia. Whenever Leah caught up with the Jake McCray story, then she could understand why Allison was locked up inside right now. If Leah didn't know by the time she came back tonight, Allison would make sure of it.

Allison waited until she heard the front door of her cabin-turned-apartment shut and click.

"*Free,*" she choked out loud before pitching her head down to her knees. Gnashing the hem of her underwear between her teeth and stuffing as much of it as she could into her mouth with two fingers to muffle herself, lest Leah hear her in the driveway, Allison screeched.

Allison had long grown used to the feverish sounds of Bright Horizons Day Care after four years on the job. The screaming, giggling, wailing, whooping, whining, crashing, banging and redirecting were all part of a daily resonance that would seem remiss to her otherwise. Allison depended upon these sounds as much as she'd depended upon the silence at home. It was her own natural balance allowing her a slow heal over the past eight years. As of yesterday, the wound had been gashed wide open.

If Leah hadn't been with her all night, Allison might have gone mad with only her thoughts to keep her company. Having the extra sleeping noises and occasional tumbling and twisting about of another person in her bed had given Allison a fleeting sense of sanctuary. Best friends served more than a purpose; they were lifelines.

Though it had been reported Jake McCray was on the other side of the country after being released from the Twin Towers Correctional Facility in Los Angeles, the petrifying thought he might come in the middle of the night, kicking down Allison's door and repeating what he'd done to her all those years ago wouldn't leave her mind. Even with Leah under the same roof, Allison had thrice considered bringing a kitchen knife into her bedroom and stashing it beneath her pillow.

Here amidst the relentless grind of a day care that would drive the parents out of their collective skulls, Allison began to calm down, just a little.

"Hunter, *no*," Allison said in a stern voice, redirecting the toddler in question from pelting Haley Williams in the head with a wooden alphabet block. There had been fewer traditional blocks at Brighter Horizons for this very reason. The director, Pam Ivers, had replaced most, but not all of them with the Pretex stackable blocks that looked like oversized Legos. They were a big hit with the threes.

"No!" Haley repeated Allison in a squeaky imitation, stretching her tiny hands out to block Hunter Reed, who looked confused by the whole thing.

"The young lady has spoken," Allison said with a faint giggle which felt tremendous right now.

Hunter took a second glance at the block in his dinky fist, then again at Haley. He raised the block once more like it was his mission to clock Haley with it.

"I said *no*, Hunter!" Allison ordered with shriller force. She opened her palm in between the two children, almost wishing *Star Wars* and The Force were a real thing. "Give it here."

Hunter gave up on Haley and instead turned to Allison with the block.

"One…" she warned him. "Two…"

This time Hunter got with the program. He leaned forward and dropped the block into Allison's hand before rocking backwards and peeling off a pleased-with-himself squeal Allison couldn't help but adore.

"Good job, bud," she told him. Haley expressed her own approval by clapping and giggling. Her hands missed one another more than connected, and the slaps sounded faint, like the pattering of a cat's paws across linoleum.

Allison had started as a teacher's aide in the one-year-olds room before being promoted to lead teacher of the twos a year later. Her co-workers had teased her, claiming it was the furthest thing from a promotion. Day care teachers were expected to be malleable for all ages ranging from infancy to age five, filling in other rooms as needed. Yet Allison had come to find the twos were nowhere near as flippant as the mouthy threes nor as untamable as the fireball fours.

Her kids were rowdy, sure. There was always justification to the term "Terrible Twos," no matter how many new enrollments came and went through Allison's room. The twos cried all the time, they were working to stop unloading in their training pants and they were still learning it wasn't okay to hit, tackle and bite one another. Yet there was a sense of normalcy to it all that made Allison's job routine in a satisfying way.

She had her bad days like anyone else at Bright Horizons and she had days where the parents were noisier than their offspring. It was often the parents who sent Allison home in a funk more so than the kids.

Allison was sometimes brought bad children who just couldn't interact with other kids in an appropriate manner. More than a few had kicked Allison, spat on her, and gnawed into her wrists.

Those kids beyond discipline were dismissed and dropped by Pam, who wasn't above tossing away tuition money if it meant keeping order in her program. Allison not only respected Pam for that, she worshipped her. Pam was strict and operated to the deepest code in the regs book. She gave none of her staff a square inch, including her brash Assistant Director and lead in the fives room, Meg Moran. Word had it Meg was one chew-out away from hitting the bricks for her recent argument with a parent. All the parent had been reported to have done was to ask Meg to keep her rambunctious kid, Jacob Weinstein away from his destructive, pre-K partner-in-crime, Emma Larson.

"Maybe it's just me," Allison said to her aide, Clarita Juarez. "I think we have the primo age. Meg can have the fives all she wants."

"Meg can have anything she wants around here," Clarita said with derision.

"Except Pam's job, though you can see her politicking around here."

"Batista's coup in Cuba worked because he had weak opposition already in power. Called the election off and declared himself dictator after sending the government out of the country to Mexico City. Just like that. History tends to repeat itself."

"A little radical," Allison said, her face wrenching from the comparison. "I doubt Meg has too great an influence with the Fleming family to coax them into firing Pam. There's no need. Pam's a hard ass, but she run this place as tight as brunch at First Watch."

"Don't be so sure," Clarita told Allison, picking up Abby Feight and carrying her to the changing table to remove a ripe diaper.

"Incoming!" Allison joked, which felt magnificent.

"To think we repeat this cycle in our old ages," Clarita cracked back.

"Lidocaine, here we come."

Allison had wrapped her arms around countless Brittanys, Aubreys, Wyatts, Coopers and Madisons in her tenure at Bright Horizons. Loving these children and watching them grow helped bury the torment of being raped by Jake McCray. She'd found her purpose, her calling. She'd given her own child to Heaven, but post-trauma, Heaven for Allison had become a suburban day care center.

The devil had come knocking at the gates, though.

With Clarita on the other end of the room attending to Abby, Allison knelt down to Hunter, who was tugging on the ankle of her jeans.

"What'cha want, trouble?"

Hunter gave Allison no answer, only another cutesy shriek, as if he'd heard the joke of a lifetime making sense only to two-year-olds.

"You can't take *this* away from me, McCray," she whispered.

Freedom felt weird.

Even weirder doing an interview after his seven years in the slammer, much less in a private condo set up for Jake McCray by The Brigadiers' longtime manager, Ron Falconio.

Jake hadn't had much time to enjoy the king-size bed, a private toilet that flushed with the water gorging upwards, and a fully stocked refrigerator with things he liked to eat and drink. Last night, his first outside of Twin Towers prison, Jake took down three bottles of a

California amber craft beer called Red Rattler and he cooked himself a bone-in ribeye steak, leaving it medium. The frozen quinoa with cranberries paired well with it. To think two nights ago, Jake had been shoving down that watery slop representing chicken pot pie with a disgusting cream looking like a spread of jackoff from the shower room floor tiles.

"After seven years, how does it feel to be on the outside?" he was asked. He'd let the journalist from PillarsofPower.com, Celine Sturm, into his temporary residence on the seventeenth floor of the Largo-Sheffield condo building in Brentwood. He'd almost forgotten she was there, though a whiff of Gucci Bloom reminded him she'd come as the first authorized press granted by Ron and his business partner and wife, Candy.

Celine Sturm kicked her right leg up and down across her left knee, shooting a traceable squeak between her thigh-high brown leather boots. She wore a black cotton skirt which kissed the mouth of the boots, and she had on a Judas Priest *Screaming for Vengeance* t-shirt, giving her only a smidge of cred in Jake's eyes. He'd read Celine Sturm's work on the web this morning while chomping on a heated sticky bun. She'd muffed the spelling of Adrian Smith in an Iron Maiden piece she'd done only a few months ago. Blame her or blame her editor for the embarrassing gaffe of *Arian* Smith.

Her first question did little to inspire Jake. It was predictable, but he also knew it was what the people wanted to know, more so the reason he'd been given a reduced sentence and early out. The Brigadiers, after completing a so-called farewell tour eight years ago, were promoting a reunion album and a support tour, featuring their sprung-free drummer.

"Well, Celine," Jake said to her, looking instead at a painting in the living room which Ron had mounted. It was ugly, full of gross greens and browns reminding him of the prison commodes or worse, the slime passing as its green bean casserole. "I'm still getting used to wearing regular clothes again, sleeping in a real bed, not a bunk, and having a choice of going to bed when I want to. I had a lights out recurrence last night at 11:00. Remember, I've only been out for a little more than a day. The prison experience is still a very real thing for me. I found myself shutting the lights off in here after watching *Storage Wars* reruns. Five minutes later, I was turning it all back on and whacking on drum pads for an hour. Sidebar, it's nice to be able to bust a nut without other dudes seeing you."

Celine laughed, but not with much starch. It seemed phony to Jake. She looked put off, especially by the line about masturbation. He shrugged inside his mind as he waited for her next question.

"Take me back to the sentencing hearing," she said, already plucking Jake's nerves. If he didn't owe Ron and Candy a debt for pulling the right strings to get him an early release, then setting him up with sweet, indefinite lodging to get his bearings, he'd tell Celine Sturm to go fuck herself all the way out the door.

"What about it?" he asked, trying to remove the stacking malice from his voice.

"They put you away for assault and drug possession."

"Like I need a reminder, Ms. Sturm?" She'd just lost the right to familiarity in Jake's eyes. In fact, it was the first time since The Brigadiers had formed where he'd addressed an interviewer in a formal manner. "Worst goddamn day of my life. What is it you want to know?"

"I just..."

"Let me save you and all future writers the trouble, so make sure you print this: I regret what I've done. I've made many mistakes in my life, things I've been held accountable for, others...well, we all fuck up at some point, don't we? I wear my crimes louder than the average person since I was in the public eye a good twenty years before I went away. I'll admit I've done things I'm not proud of by any stretch of the imagination. I'm sure there's things I did I'll never even remember. If you'd ever played seriously in a major league rock 'n roll band, you'd know I'm talking about."

"Do you want to be absolved of it all, Jake? Do you view your release from jail as a chance at possible redemption?"

"Did you come with any music-topical questions, Ms. Sturm? If not, I'll end this interview with a final statement, and I won't give it again, that's a promise. Prison has a way of changing people. I'm a changed man. The Brigadiers are reforming. I'm an integral part of the equation, which includes a new album and upcoming tour. I was a complete asshole before prison. I ain't about to go back there from being that same asshole."

It felt like eight years ago, though Allison knew it wasn't.

She knew it wasn't because she was holding hands with her old boyfriend, Bradley Padgett. It was a sticky summer night in downtown Atlanta, the kind of hectoring dinnertime heat lending itself to evening baseball at Turner Field, but obnoxious for concert-going. All the changes which had occurred in eight long, yet scary quick years, including a new stadium for the Braves sponsored by SunTrust Bank.

Having closed a few years back, its demise was mourned more by Atlanta Gen-Xer headbangers and punks than anyone from her own generation. Allison cheered out loud over a chocolate chip waffle and a greasy plate of bacon when she'd read of Anarchy, Inc.'s closure. She'd never forget the breakfast, nor that article. An unexpected relief to her, the club's finish represented closure for Allison with Jake McCray serving his sentence on the opposite side of the country. As the inadvertent scene of the crime, Allison hardly hated to see it go, despite a long scroll of melancholy rock scene mourners posting their memories and well-wishes on the club's website.

For its worth, at the time, Allison had cared for Bradley. So much that she'd agreed to go with him to Anarchy, Inc., one of the most fateful decisions of her life, aside from the abortion. As Allison's poor luck would have it, the *reason* for the abortion.

Allison could see herself in her ground-scuffing jeans with the frayed tatters skating around her ankles. Nobody in her age bracket wore bell-bottoms, but Allison had always been wired against the grain. They often caught under her feet and caused her to stagger, though she hadn't yet started drinking then, even a full year legal. Allison had also been wearing a rescued gray and white checked flannel shirt of her deceased father's, put into a donation box by her mother for Goodwill. Allison had worshipped her dad. The shirt was one way of keeping a connection to him.

Even in the low nineties that evening, Allison wore the masculine flannel shirt because Bradley also wore them. Seldom few collegiates outside of engineering and agricultural majors wore flannel button downs on campus at Kennesaw. As it happened, Bradley *was* an engineering major.

Since Bradley was about to graduate ahead of her, they'd decided they were going to break up at some point, though agreeing to milk what they'd built in nearly a year together. Allison's time at the university would continue another two years despite the pressure put upon her by her curriculum counselor to accelerate her semesters with full-time course loads.

Even when Bradley didn't ask Allison to join him on his future move to McLean, Virginia, she hadn't taken offense. His proposal to make things an open relationship was a different story, since the thought of Bradley getting it on with other coeds she might chance by on campus didn't sit right with Allison. Her ultimatum had been exclusivity until they'd decided upon a clean break.

Their romance had been fun, dreamy at times, but there hadn't been too much of a connection between them. He liked sports; she preferred The Atlanta Contemporary Art Center (where you got free coffee to wander and gaze with) and the Mason Murer Fine Art Gallery. They'd made out a lot, even went all the way once. Bradley had been sweet with her after breaking her hymen. Allison had spotted the next two days and never let him get that far again. She'd thanked her lucky stars she'd made him wear a condom then.

Mostly they'd hung out, by themselves and with Bradley's friends or Leah or a combination. He spun only music he liked, never Ani DiFranco, Tori Amos, or Fiona Apple, all of whom Allison and Leah shared a passion for. He liked heavy music, which was harder on the ears in Allison's opinion than political debates. The relationship had become a stuck mojo in a hurry, and yet Allison found herself agreeing to accompany Bradley to Anarchy, Inc., the night she'd been raped.

Bradley's brother Carl worked as a concert promoter and he'd arranged for the two to attend a meet-and-greet backstage with The Brigadiers, who were co-headlining a club tour with L.A. Guns on their purported farewell tour. Both bands had hit their heights of stardom back in the Eighties and both had fallen from their glam metal pedestals. Though neither Allison nor Bradley cared about The Brigadiers or L.A. Guns, Allison remembered both being big-time draws of their era. Plus, a backstage pass was a backstage pass. It would be something to talk about if she and Bradley ever crossed paths again in life. As it was, the venue had struggled to push tickets prior to the event but sold out on game night.

"Should be interesting," Bradley's voice echoed inside Allison's mind as they held hands waiting outside of the club. The hand holding had been mere formality, as Allison dwelled upon it. A going-through the motions.

Bradley had a hidden high alto peeking through the mid-level virility of his voice. When the alto came out, Bradley sounded bitchy. This was one of those moments and though they were destined for breakup, the bitchy speak and the clamminess of Bradley's tight grip was something Allison was feeling all over again in recollection of it.

The longer they remained outside waiting to be escorted into the meet-and-greet, the more Allison began to sweat underneath that incubating flannel. Much later that evening, it would be shoved into the trash can behind her house. She'd wanted to burn it first, but instead apologized to her father in the afterlife under her breath, hoping he understood the circumstances as to why. It would become unwearable anyway.

In the rear lot of Anarchy, Inc., Allison started flapping the flannel above her chest in the hopes of fanning a self-contained cool breeze, since there was nothing to grab out of the humid air around them. It didn't help the stench of garbage and piss behind the club choked what little good oxygen there was. She'd never forget that dynamic as she'd never forget every horrifying moment afterwards.

"Sorry, Bradley," she said to him, shaking free of his hand and undoing the first three buttons of the shirt. They would never hold hands again afterwards. "This heat's getting to me." She hadn't been wearing a bra, but the sweat slicking her sternum and dripping between her cleavage had at least provoked the proper amount of compassion from Bradley. Besides, once she let the folds of the shirt rest, it didn't offer much of a view of her then-size Cs. She'd been thirty pounds lighter.

"It's going to be hard saying goodbye to the girls," she remembered Bradley joking to her. She also remembered groaning to herself over it as much as the frequency in which the juvenile tit goblin snuck up from behind to honk her.

Once backstage in one of two dressing rooms reserved for the club's scheduled talent, they'd shaken hands with The Brigadiers, who looked bored out of their minds, more interested in getting to the beer and the cheese spread the venue had put out for them than hobnobbing with their guests. The guitarist they called "Shredder" was the most social but all he did was cuss up a storm, while the bassist Chaz Childress snorted like a wart hog in intervals at the mini gathering of eight invitees. The L.A. Guns crew had the other dressing room and if they were entertaining guests as well, they'd been far more silent about their business.

The lead singer, Garen Stone, had the other three girls in the party (all in their mid-twenties) circumventing him, begging him for pictures and pushing up the slopes of their jangly hooters for him to sign with a magic marker. Stone obliged them all, but there was a hapless sense of ennui to it. He struck rock god poses for their cell cameras, waggled his tongue, and took what appeared to be an entire portfolio of digital shots with those girls clawing on him, showing off the streaked magic marker across their chests. One of the girls had been bold enough to push her butt against his crotch and clamped Garen's hand to her left breast, while her boyfriend took the shot. The boyfriend looked as excited about it as she did. Stone began running his thumb across her nipple until it got hard enough to poke through her shirt, which prompted a lot of squealing and laughter from the other guests, save for Allison. She'd grown immediately pissed at Bradley's enjoyment of the whole scene. Stone looked he was merely *there*, his carnal act a mere daily-do.

Then there was Jake McCray.

After saying his noncommittal hellos, McCray had sidled up next to Chaz Childress and both were pulling on beers. Allison would never forget how the bottle tipped to McCray's lips and, emptied in seconds, twirled in the air, shattering against the nearest wall. McCray had ripped a monstrous belch which got everyone but her laughing. He'd repulsed Allison upon sight. Bradley had been impressed by the duration of the burp. Of course he'd been.

Because she wasn't laughing, Jake McCray pinpointed Allison and scouted — no, *hunted* was the better word — for her eyes.

His were dark brown and Allison had thought McCray's grim pupils were malevolent, scarier than Charles Manson's, whom she'd always thought had demon's eyes every time those forensics shows on Discovery Channel ran one of their profiles on him. She'd grown uncomfortable once McCray had caught her gaze. Part of his stare was magnetic, despite the insinuated wickedness behind them. She wasn't attracted to him, not in the least. Disgusted as Allison was with Jake McCray, she was still compelled to stare back.

"Shredder" Cook had joined Garen Stone as one of the other girls handed off her cell phone to one of her friends before nestling inside Shredder's arm, her hand resting across his belly. Allison could still hear Shredder tell the girl to go lower in joking, and yet she did. One of her friends took the picture as Shredder popped wood through his latex and they all howled, the rest wanting in for a group photo. Aging rockers well into their fifties, acting like it was 1985 all over again. Allison was about to tell Bradley she wanted to leave, even if she had to call a cab back to campus. In retrospect, she wished she'd done so. It had been her only chance.

Bradley was asked by the guy with the cell if he minded taking over so the dudes could get into the shots. Allison recalled nearly lashing out her hand and sinking her fingernails into Bradley's arm to hold him in place, because Jake McCray was heading in her direction.

Bradley was in his own world and growing turned on by it. He shook free of her. Again, that word, *free.* Allison would never look at Bradley the same way again.

He'd broken away from her and was already pressing click on the cell camera while the three girls, now joined by their male counterparts, were mugging it up with The Brigadiers, most of them muscle flexing, pumping their fists or flashing the horns-up salute. One couple got outright daring and simulated a pumping from behind standing sexual position in the center of it all. Shredder pawed at the girl who'd grabbed his crotch and tugged her loose shirt up for one of the pictures. Like Allison, she'd been wearing no bra. Instead of getting pissed, her boyfriend cheered with delight as he and Shredder each grabbed one of the freed breasts. Delirious by the prospect of a rock orgy, she plunged her hand down Shredder's tights and unzipped her boyfriend at the same time.

Bradley whispered "Holy shit" at it all as he snapped away. "Can I text these to myself?" he'd asked as someone still in high school who's never scored would. This wasn't the same guy Allison had come to know. He wasn't the one for her, it had already been established, but he'd been charming for much of the time. He knew the lost art of holding doors for ladies, a point once added, now wiped from Allison's ledger on him. This shameful display and his selfish disregard for her own welfare undid any and all of his good deeds.

"You guys want to take this on our bus?" Shredder asked, which prompted a whoop from all the company except for Allison.

Jake McCray, oblivious to the decadence around them, had crossed the room and was within feet of Allison.

"How ya doin' honey?" he'd asked her. She could still smell the beer on his breath and see the moist pallor of his skin. His brown shag had been longer in the Eighties but now it was crimped back with a silver headband way out of fashion.

"Hey, camera guy, follow us!"

Allison remembered watching Bradley filter out of the room with the party, leaving behind knocked over beer bottles and wiped-out cheese platters. Bradley, the rat, hadn't even checked on her. He'd been so enthralled by the moment Allison hadn't crossed his mind again as the dressing room door closed behind him. Their breakup came right then and there, only he wouldn't know it until the next day.

"You're a fine young thing," McCray had said, reaching out to touch Allison's jumbled locks. "The Pearl Jam look's fucking sloppy, though. Normally, flannel's a turnoff for me, but whatever, it's been a long tour. Beggars can't be choosers."

Allison pulled her head back a few inches as terror spread throughout her. The rest of her became paralyzed. It was as if the mere touch of his fingers to her hair held the power of immobilization.

"No," she'd said in a frightened, squeaky voice. Once and only once, but it had been issued.

With only she and Jake McCray left in the dressing room, she was more fearful of the potential of what could happen than what *did* happen.

He'd been so fast she hadn't yet realized he'd ripped the remaining buttons of the flannel shirt free. The chilly, grubby waft from the air conditioning sprinkled goosebumps all over her skin. Not until she heard the echoing *plink-plink-plink* of those detached buttons on the floor did Allison realize she was in trouble.

"Darlin' those puppies are beautiful," she heard McCray say and still it hadn't fully registered what was happening to her until she felt his mouth on her right nipple. For a shocking second, an actual shiver of pleasure tickled her pelvis. Remembering *that* nauseated Allison many times over the years.

The unexpected and unwanted tingle coursing throughout Allison's body splintered away as McCray unfastened her jeans faster than she could process it. An expert from years of sex on the road, his greedy hand was already entrenched inside her pubic hair, tugging the curls through his fingers. Allison gasped aloud as not one, but two scratchy, nail-sharpened fingers savagely pushed into her.

"Come on, honey, give daddy some sugar before everyone else gets back," he'd said, continuing to probe the most secretive place on Allison's body.

She remembered shrieking then swinging for McCray's face. She'd missed by inches. She remembered shouting Bradley's name. He never came back.

"Spunky," McCray said with less saccharine and more determination to have his way with her.

As if predetermined she would lose, Alison found herself face down on a grubby brown sofa that smelled like dust and flatulence. McCray was so instantaneous with his maneuvers it took Allison a moment to know through her stark terror he'd ripped her naked out of her clothes. He was so dreadfully strong.

All she remembered then was the pain. Lots of it. It seemed like McCray would never be done. Allison sobbed and yelped into the sofa as he took her. She only had enough oxygen coming into the corner of her sticky, unctuous mouth flooding from her tears. He was hard and mean, yielding no ounce of tenderness. The more she heard the echoing smack of his crotch against her bottom, the more humiliating it was.

Then he bit into her shoulder and grumbled like a gorilla as his pelvis shuddered. Her butt was already jiggling from his feral thrusts, but then he dug his fingers into the flesh of her hips as he came inside of her. Those fingernails... Jesus, they were almost as harsh as his penis.

She screamed as she felt his release coat her insides. Worse, he shoved her head down into the sofa to muffle her.

To reflect upon it now was to be violated all over again.

"Welcome to the big leagues, sweetheart," McCray had mocked, slamming into her some more before coming a second time. Only then did he pull out, leaving Allison cold and naked on that disgusting couch. The sound of his zipper going up was the final noise she could recollect, aside from Jake telling her she had VIP all night if she wanted another round after the show.

Allison…Allison…

"Hey, honey, wake up…"

The voice was feminine. Leah. *Thank God,* it was Leah. That horrific day wasn't truly happening again. Allison thought God seldom listened to her, but she thanked Him nonetheless as she opened her eyes and found herself in her own bed, her drenched head inside of Leah's lap.

"Man, you must've had a whopper of a dream, Ally," Leah said, streaming her fingers through Allison's damp follicles. The bedroom was dark, but the hallway light had been left on and Allison could see Leah's warm smile. She was wearing a baggy gray sweatshirt she'd packed for tonight and a flappity pair of men's boxers. Ever since Allison had known Leah, her best friend had been fond of sleeping in those ridiculous boxers.

Allison's cheek was hot and sweaty pressed against Leah's lap, but she wanted more warmth, and she latched her arms around Leah's waist.

"You kept saying something along the lines of 'big leagues' or some weirdness like that. What in the world did you dream?"

Allison's body shuddered. She could once again feel the fierce jabbing of Jake McCray inside her. He was *so big,* she remembered. He'd torn her, a pain lasting well beyond the healing. How could she ever forget?

It had happened so long ago, but Allison was flustered believing Jake had broken into her place and ravished her a second time, right now, eight years from the first. She hurt down there this very minute, phantom aching from forced entry long ago.

The monster who'd done it to her was on the loose again.

Allison pulled Leah closer to her, smothering her face into Leah's flat belly. Then Allison yelped into Leah's guts, writhing with her tears.

"Oh my God, Ally," Leah gasped. The sudden clutching, shivering, and sobbing made Leah lean down and wrap herself around Allison. "What's wrong, you poor baby? What happened? Something at the day care?"

Allison's squeaks turned to screeches cast into Leah's abdomen. Her body wracked from the exertion, much as Leah tried to soothe her.

"Shhhh," Leah comforted. "Come on, Ally, calm down. Shh, baby, shhhhhh... I'm here. Did that Meg bitch from work do something to you?"

"N-no," Allison stammered, sliding her moist cheek against Leah's stomach, drying at least half of her face in the process.

"Then what? Ally, I've never seen you like this, not since...oh, no, don't tell me."

"They let him out."

"Nobody wants to talk about the new record and the tour, Ron," Jake groused into a cell phone which had been activated the same day of his release from Twin Towers. A brand-new droid, which meant as much to Jake as C-3P0 and his rolling shit bucket pal making all of its squirrely beeps from its spinning dome.

The fact Jake had his own phone and a place to live without bars and angry, tatted dudes in his face, *that's* what counted on his second day of freedom. A bed to stretch out in didn't hurt, either. It felt more liberating than sex. He could spread his limbs from the middle of this bed into an "X" position and not even touch the sides. The master bedroom bath was many feet away instead of inches, and it smelled clean. Not as if a hundred apes had defecated in it.

Jake recollected the king-sized beds The Brigadiers used to command at the nicest hotels on each stop of their itinerary in the glory days. It was one of the band's touring stipulations, king-size beds, no smaller. Then there was Garen's outrageous demand—prima donna that he was—of a Mr. Goodbar to be placed not only at each hotel stop with his name written on it, but in each dressing room. This to make sure everyone in the band and crew knew it was *his* goddamn candy bar.

The one time a Mr. Goodbar had been neglected to be left at some arena in St. Louis long razed and rebuilt, Garen had trashed the dressing room. He demanded the venue send someone to fetch him a Mr. Goodbar, threatening not to go onstage until then. It was when record labels had the money to pamper their artists, albeit the only ones afforded such luxuries were the ones making double their advances from album sales. The era of coddling and ludicrous extravagances was gone, including the spineless venue executives with their stand-by gophers to cater to such excessive whims. Most who lived them who weren't a band manager called them *the good old days*.

"Just hang in there, Jake," he heard Ron tell him through the droid phone, a current model Samsung Galaxy. Ron had seen to so much for Jake, it was the good old days returned. "Part and parcel, you know. People want dirt because they're bored. They don't see the bigger picture. We're working on a rebrand here, The Brigadiers and a reformed Jake McCray."

"It's only the reform they want to know about," Jake said, staring at the ceiling.

Before he'd been arrested for mashing the teeth out of the officer who'd arrested him while taking a whiz in that parking garage on South La Cienega in Inglewood, Jake would've wanted a bump. The idea of snorting cocaine right now made Jake queasy thinking about it, as much as how he'd felt on his way to Twin Towers in that awful transport van, the sweat box.

The ride to prison was even worse than the strip search and the intrusive probing in the BOSS chair. More humiliating than the laundry list questions designed to see if Jake was a suicide threat. This before the overpowering list of prison rules and consequences, the "compacts," the inmates called it. The biscuits and orange squash drink Jake had received at the end of intake were the only amenities provided that horrible day. A far cry from a Mr. Goodbar.

"Candy had your old kit pulled from storage and set up in the studio when you're ready," Ron told him. "It's been a few years."

"Yeah, it has," Jake said, running his fingers over chiseled abs from the open section of a velvet silk rope Ron had provided. Special-ordered out of Italy, he'd made sure to brag. 58 years old, the last seven spent in a cage, Jake had no business looking as good as did. About the only thing he liked doing in prison more than watching the tube and writing the bad poetry he'd thrown out was pumping weights in the exercise yard.

"Nobody's expecting a miracle off-the-bat, so keep hitting on the drum pads over there until your chops are up."

"I'm almost goddamn sixty, Ron. *Don't* expect a miracle."

"And rock 'n roll's almost as dead as we are," Ron gibed, prompting bare minimum laughter between them.

"You speak to Dana lately? How's she doing?"

"Beats the hell out of me, Jake. I don't keep tabs on your ex. After your divorce went final, she went off the grid. Nobody knows where she went. She sold the house in Burbank, closed all her social media and blocked Candy and I from her phone. That's all I've got for you."

"Alright, man," Jake said, feeling his first sense of defeat since he'd left prison.

"You remember the video shoot for 'Morality Killer', Jake?" Ron asked, the gravity of his query pounding through the phone into Jake's ears.

"Not really, man," Jake sighed. "I had a doobie in my mouth every time the director called action. Take after take, all for a lousy three seconds of me laying down a tom roll then pointing my stick into the camera. Such crap. I was wasted for most of it."

"Yeah, I know. We *all* knew, including Dana."

"She was there?"

"Long enough to catch you deep-throating the mic boom girl between set-ups. That's where it all went off the rails for you, Jake."

"Christ, I don't even remember it."

"Take my word for it, pal. It happened. Dana has a stronger constitution than Candy. If it had been me, she would've castrated me right on the shoot in front of everybody. Dana recorded video of the sword-swallowing bit. You're stoned out of your damn mind in that clip, and you're guilty as hell. I paid Dana a fortune not to leak it. We agreed she would only use it to divorce you and so far, she's made good on our agreement. I love you to death, Jake, but you had it coming. All of it."

"Yeah, I did," Jake said in stale, sober voice before swiping the call disconnect.

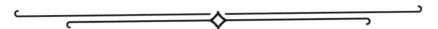

Doing Circle Time was more a chore than usual. Like the day before, Allison's belly punched at her while she organized her kids into an awkward semblance of a semicircle around her to read *Goodnight, Moon* to them. Not one of her kids stayed in place and it took extra patience on her part this morning to direct and redirect them through the story.

She was happy she'd chosen such a short book, because today her twos just weren't having it. Neither was Allison.

Even Clarita seemed on the verge of popping when Tyrone Marks stepped on Faith Herndon's hand in a toddler-styled dispute over a Tonka truck. Both kids let loose noisome bawling pricking Allison's nerves for just a moment before she separated them. In that moment, she allowed an uncharacteristic rumination vent through her wracked mind: *You kids have no reason to cry like this. You're not even old enough to know what* real *pain is.*

As it was with her yesterday, Allison's bladder had stored up and locked the gates on her. If she didn't relieve herself soon, Allison might surrender to the intolerance building inside her. The more she struggled to pee, the angrier it was making her. She'd cursed Jake McCray's name to herself all morning long.

"You don't look so hot," Clarita said to Allison, carrying a tube of ointment while reaching for Faith's reddened, smarting hand. "What's wrong?"

"I'm not sleeping too well this week," Allison answered in a low pitch. It wasn't a lie, but she wasn't about to get into her problems any further.

Though Allison didn't want to spend long minutes she didn't have inside the teacher's rest room, she was getting downright sick. To make matters worse, her head was mounting a fierce attack against her. It had been a dull thump before Tyrone and Faith had nearly peeled the yellow paint off the walls with their shrieks. Now it was inflicting massive throbs from Allison's brain and sending pulses into her guts — sharing the wealth between each other.

Pam's office was close to the teacher's bathroom, which only added to Allison's trepidation. Pam was a fair boss most of the time, but she could be a pain with teachers who were out of their rooms longer than necessary. Aides were there for backup, but not to take over for full lengths of time. Pam always cited state codes and regulations to her staff as reminders to keep their room counts in compliance with appropriate ratios of staff to children.

In ten minutes, Allison would need to begin lunch prep. This would put Clarita temporarily in charge of the nine kids who were already jacked up. The noisy antics of Tyrone and Faith had become contagious amongst the other kids, Hunter especially. He'd been more of a screamer than a giggler today. Getting them all down for nap time was going to be a challenge, Allison predicted.

That wasn't for another forty-five minutes, and Allison preferred to hit the bathroom after the kids were asleep. She wasn't sure she could hold out that long. All the times Allison urged her children to holler out when they needed to go potty was full-on irony to her. She might wet herself any minute now and she would feel hypocritical any time she turned a child toward the kids' toilet and coax its usage like a "big" boy or girl.

"Clarita," she said, finally surrendering to her protesting body. She held her belly for added effect. "I'm so sorry, but I'm going to bust if I don't go to the ladies' room."

"I got it," the young aide said bravely, though Allison could see a brief flicker of panic from her hazel pupils. As if she was going into battle,

Clarita fished out a hair scrunchie looking like an oversized inchworm, then swept her raven tresses into a sloppy ponytail. Clarita's game face rang more of self-preservation.

"Thank you," Allison said, patting Clarita on the shoulder. "I'm going to hurl if I don't go."

Clarita said nothing back. She entered the fray of bobbling, gabbing two-year-olds with admirable courage.

Mercifully, Allison was able to go this time. It was long and pleasant, as if such a thing could be had right now. Her stomach began to ease, and her bladder cooled, though it still raked her for making it work overtime. As she washed her hands afterwards, Allison noticed in the mirror her cheeks had flushed and she was carrying faint black bags underneath her eyes. It was the mark of exhaustion, more attributable to people in their forties and beyond, not a woman still in her twenties.

"*You* did this to me, you bastard," she whispered before dashing out of the bathroom and hurrying back to the twos room. She'd breezed by Pam, who half-smiled and half-frowned at her from the doorway to her office.

"Three minutes makes a world of difference whether Licensing shuts us down or not," Pam needled at Allison.

"Yes, ma'am," Allison said back, double-timing her steps.

Not even *three minutes,* Allison moaned to herself as she swung back into the twos room. Inside, Clarita looked like a junior female Gulliver about to be toppled to the floor with all nine toddlers herded around her ankles. Laurie Berkner was chirping from the room's portable CD player, crooning about feeling so crazy Berkner would jump in a soup. The kids were jumping with Berkner and about to take Clarita into the supposed soup with them.

"Boooooogies!" Tyrone beeped at Allison upon seeing her, holding out his right middle and forefingers smeared by his own snot.

"Give me strength," Allison muttered for more than one reason.

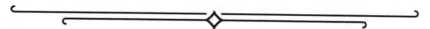

Leah offered to stay with Allison a third night now that she was on-point about the recent developments with Jake McCray. During the kids' nap time, Allison sent Leah a quick text saying she wanted to be alone tonight. She was sorry she did.

In the shower, Allison let the hot water grab and slide down her skin. It was the first thing she did every workday, to purge herself of the reek of kid caca and barf and the sometimes-unbearable cling of bleach and disinfectant.

The bathroom filled with steam and Allison sucked it all in, trying to cleanse her insides as much her exterior. The clouding vapor opened her lungs, ridding her of the foul aftertaste of Mr. Croker's cigarettes which slammed into her in the mere minute she'd been exposed to it. She'd gone up to the manor upon her arrival home to ask Dru if it was okay she was having regular company, since Allison had been otherwise alone since moving in. Allison and Leah usually met at Leah's place or elsewhere whenever they hung out. After Dru told Allison not to worry, there'd been no other exchange between them between a thank you and a sullen nod in response. Allison could hear Mr. Croker's brackish coughing from somewhere in the manor. He sounded like he was being branded by something hotter than a cigarette.

The scalding shower soaked deep into Allison's pores, relaxing her for the first time in the past couple days, if only for a fleeting moment.

She couldn't take her mind off it.

Jake McCray was out there, and Allison was scared.

Right now, she was trembling as she glided the soap bar down her abdomen, beneath the folds of her sopping breasts, along her slippery hips. She was about to wash down below, then, as if jolted through the water, she recoiled from it.

The events again replayed in her mind as the steam built and coated the bathroom mirror. Her lungs praised her, yet her belly quaked once again and her vagina twitched, as angry as the rest of her. Would it have been worse if she'd been able to *see* Jake raping her? If Allison thought she'd cried herself out the past two days, she was wrong. The tears came again. This time out of fury instead of sorrow and self-pity.

She thought about calling Leah after she was done cleaning up, but she didn't want her friend to see her like this. Maybe tomorrow if she could get a grip. The only satisfaction Allison took right now was feeling more resolved than afraid. Outraged instead of disgraced.

"I want you gone for good," she said, the spray of the boiling water bouncing off her drenched lips. Her skin was reddening and now the pain seeped in. It was as if Jake McCray was in the shower with her right now, bending her over and taking her once more.

Never again, she swore right there and then.

Verbally, she vowed, "Whatever it takes. *Gone.*"

"Whoever designed this page ought to be fired," Leah groaned in dismissal. "Made to do the Walk of Shame, *then* fired. I've seen blogs with better interface than this. The CMS is so primary a teenager might've coded it."

"What's that?" Allison asked, taking a sip of Chardonnay from one of a pair of wine glasses Dru had given her as a housewarming gift. It took everything she had inside her wrist to keep the glass steady.

"Content Management System," Leah answered in a blasé manner, trying not to let her irritation with The Brigadiers' website get the better of her. "The JavaScript doesn't work well, nor the HTML functions. I can tell you right now those are the reasons for the slow loading. It can't be for access overload. Who the hell cares about this dinosaur band anymore? Definitely not their IT."

"Enough of a dinosaur band to make the national news," Allison said in a flat tone.

"Maybe some time spent with Behance might speed the damn thing up," Leah chattered.

"Okay, we've established their website sucks, Leah. Does it have the upcoming tour dates?"

"Yeah, let me load it up for you and then be my guest."

Leah rose from the swiveling, leather-backed office chair at Allison's pressboard desk and gestured for her to take a seat. The chair, like that old flannel shirt Jake McCray had destroyed, had also belonged to her dad.

"A lot of places I've never heard of on the west coast," Allison said in a calmer state as she scrolled and took inventory. "Then they go across the northern United States, some dates in the mid-Atlantic. Places called Jasmine's, Frost Castle, Metal Nouveau, Gary Finnegan's, The Bearded Clam, seriously? Total Recool—oy, that's even worse."

"A long fall from grace out of the arenas."

Allison scrolled again with slow finger swipes on the rolling mouse. thirty-eight total announced dates for The Brigadiers' upcoming American reunion tour, nothing across the southern spectrum at first, but another swipe, and then...

"Aha," Allison said, half with excitement and half with dread. "They're coming to Savannah in five months."

"Rat Race?" Leah derided with a scrunched face. "That place only holds up to nine hundred max. I saw Lonnie Barber play there last summer and he only drew a couple dozen people, if that. The Brigadiers are playing that hole in the wall? Jesus."

"It was one step above a bar when Jake McCray did what he did to me," Allison reminded Leah. She surprised herself how composed she sounded right now.

"Granted," Leah said. "So, this is a speculative conversation. We know The Brigadiers are playing their first show in Austin, Texas at that big hootenanny Hollywood's claimed for itself now, South by Southwest. It'll be a while before they get to Savannah. Even a tiny dump like Rat Race will fill up in a hurry, so what do you want from this, Ally? Are you looking to confront him? I'm not sure how you'd pull it off without having credentials to get anywhere close to Jake McCray, much less take him down. I know you don't have the money, but I reiterate what I did when it happened…find some hungry lawyer fresh out of Stanford or Columbia who'd take your case cheap or at least not charge you until you win. Ally, he raped you, for Christ's sake! It didn't happen to me, and *I* want him to suffer! Why should the son of a bitch go free, other than the obvious? The Brigadiers want a cash grab and they need him to get it."

"Look, here's a contact prompt to their management," Allison said with a hint of impatience. Her friend meant well, but to do as Leah asked of her, Ally would have to go public. All these years later, Allison was still ashamed of the whole thing. Ashamed of herself for even letting Bradley take her to The Brigadiers show. She'd never told him what Jake McCray had done to her. She hadn't even told her parents. Only Leah. To drag it all out now after so much time…

"You *do* want revenge," Leah said instead of asked.

"Yes," Allison answered as she dragged the cursor over and clicked on it. Faster than anything else, a blank message form appeared, addressing new correspondence to brigadiersmgmt@powerhouse-recs.com.

Jake stomped down on the kick pedals a few times, reminding himself to lighten up the pressure in his ankles and let the toes do the work. He alternated his feet, planting the pedal to each floor tom back and forth. It wasn't so much the old adage about riding a bike, but after seven years, it took 58-year-old Jake McCray only a few tries to lay down a fluid double hammer beat, each bass drum whumping like a rapid fire metronome. He picked up speed, thinking of the intro to "Bombs Away," from The Brigadiers' second album, *Last in Lost Angeles*. It had been the opening number to the band's live sets for years, a warm-up for Jake's purposes to calibrate his legs and ankles for The Brigadiers' standard hour forty set with a fifteen-minute encore. It also fired up the crowd better than that stupid running track of the theme to *The Munsters* the band always came onstage to.

"Nice," he complimented himself as he laid down snare and hi-hat strikes between the revolving bass drums. Satisfied, he switched his right drumstick about 20 degrees, where a 22-inch Zildjian thin low ride cymbal clanged with a pleasing chime beneath the tip of Jake's gamboling taps.

He pictured a series of pyro charges erupting around his old drum cage during the 1987 tour for *Dance Sleazy*. Any other forum but a rock concert would've given the impression a war had broken out. He saw the crowd springing to its feet, sending their tidal wave of manmade thunder back at the band. The green, purple, and blue laser effects, slashing from the stage to the arena rafters. The band name BRIGADIERS lit up in a sequence of bulbs that felt hot across Jake's bare back the heavier it flashed the audience. Garen Stone dividing the squalling crowd with a gesture of his hand and motioning with a cupped ear for the left side to cheer louder than the right, and vice versa. The people ate that shit up; it was fucking glorious.

Jake saw the rise of his left stick, twirling between his left fingers before coming back to the snare on the downbeat. He'd copied the trick from Dino Danelli of The Rascals. Tommy Lee of Motley Crue was far faster than Jake; sure, there was no arguing it. Yet, Jake's spin and strike bit was made prominent in The Brigadiers' video for "She's Got Me," earning Jake a fan-voted Drummer of the Year Award in *Hit Parader* magazine.

With only Jake inside the studio now, he decided to try his luck with a stick twirl for fun. Whereas everything else had come together fast after so long a layoff, the left drumstick propelled out of his hand, spinning across the studio and bouncing off the Plexiglas window separating the musicians' pit from the recording consoles.

"Dumbass," he chided himself with a chuckle, laying down a wicked blast beat with his feet before stopping.

"Jake," he heard, piped into the studio from the recording booth.

"Jesus, Ron, how long have you been there?"

"We've got a problem," the irate manager sniped at him from the console intercom.

Jake could see the anger streaked all over Ron's face. It was as if The Brigadiers had lost their contract with Powerhouse Records as fast as it had come. The first thing Ron had Jake do before giving him the keys to the condo was to sign his name, committing to a one record deal, with future consideration based on sales.

"What, man?"

"I was reviewing the messages from the website. There's a mixed bag of people for and against the reunion. None of that matters. What does is this one email I got. The website developer even saw it. The *label reps* saw it, Jake, since all online correspondence comes through their server. She didn't give her full name. She only signed it as 'Ally from Atlanta.'"

"Okay, so how does this affect me?"

"More than you know," Ron snarled, waving a piece of paper in his hand as if he wanted to obliterate it. "I printed it out so I could read it to you. I wish it was something harder so I can slap you silly with it."

For the first time since setting foot on the asphalt outside the gates of Twin Towers, Jake felt apprehensive.

"What the hell, Ron, I..."

"Shut up. It reads, 'Eight years ago you raped me, Jake McCray," Ron read, pausing to send Jake a stink face, making him more fearsome than his 71 years would suggest. "Face down on a dirty sofa at Anarchy, Inc. That meet-and-greet was more like stealing from a stranger. How do you suppose the victim feels when you take something as precious as her body? It was the worst day of my life. I still live it. Maybe I should've sought professional counseling, but what you did was beyond humiliating. You scarred me. There's no therapist who can undo the damage you inflicted upon me. I thanked God every day for two weeks when they put you away, but now, you got out sooner than you deserved. You rock gods think you're all so special you can do whatever you want because of your celebrity. I never was a fan of The Brigadiers and I hope your upcoming tour tanks before you ever make it to Savannah.'"

Jake froze on his drum stool, feeling the first sense of actual distress since getting the separation agreement and divorce papers from Dana in prison.

"'What you stole from me I can never get back," Ron read on. "You may not remember me since you never asked my name. You may not remember what you did, but you put your despicable seed in me, you animal. I wasn't about to raise the child of a sadist I didn't even know. I kept things quiet and gave it back to God, so you don't have to worry about any paternity suits. The Christian part of me nearly kept it, though. I cried just as hard over the abortion. You screwed me good, but you know what? Screw *you*, Jake McCray. I *was* starting to get on with my life, but I can't with you out of jail. I'll be damned if I let you hurt another woman on the road, or anywhere, again. Watch your back out there.'"

"Ron, I…"

"The songs are written, the studio time is booked. I called in many favors to make this deal happen. Getting you an early parole hearing was one. Getting Sammy Hart to produce this record was another. Grammy goddamn Sammy! Is even one word of this accusation true, Jake?"

Jake squeezed his eyes closed and he dropped his head to stare at his bare feet on the kick pedals, no longer feeling like playing.

"Yes," he whispered.

"What was that?" Ron demanded.

"Yes," Jake repeated himself louder. "I remember her."

"One of the many times you cheated on Dana and worse, you *raped* this poor woman? Fuck me, Jake, what kind of a grey bar hotel degenerate are you? She's right. They should never have let you out."

"You had a hand in it, Ron."

"Don't even try me, you hypocrite. My conscience is clear, and it'll be clearer in the weeks upcoming. The rest of the guys will be here in less than an hour. I gave you an earlier arrival time so we could have this little chat. Consider it off-the-record. The band doesn't need to know, though lips leak and mouths repeat. You know how it goes in this town."

"Damn," Jake muttered.

"The condo and everything in it, you can keep. I've already signed the deed into your name and had it filed with the county recorder. My gift to you for making me and Candy millions in better times. By contract, you must play on the new Brigadiers' album. You'll fulfill your obligation and record with the band, for which I'll see you're well-compensated. Consider it an unspoken agreement between you and me that ends with you leaving the band once your parts are done. You'll make a formal announcement to the press and say whatever you want but the truth. From there, I never want to see you again."

"Come on, Ron," Jake pleaded. "I'm a new man, I..."

"Tell that to your prey in Atlanta, you worm. I doubt she's going to hear you out, and this tour can't be sabotaged over a potential stalker. I'm not disillusioned, Jake. The Big Eighties are over, but we can all still reap a modest profit from this. It would've been better with a full original member lineup, but to hell with logic; the rest us don't need this kind of publicity. I've already contacted Billy Dozier from Rawk Skewl to take your place on the tour. Remember they opened for The Brigadiers on the *Last in Lost Angeles* tour? He knows the songs. He's a good fit and Garen vouches for him."

"Sure, he would," Jake grumbled. "They tag-teamed some laced-out chick on our bus back in the day and videotaped the whole thing. Like Garen's been some kind of saint all these years."

"You of all people, Jake," Ron said, his loathing separated by Plexiglas.

Not even a full week after Jake McCray's release from prison had turned Allison's world upside down, she was gleaming in front of the television. She and Leah had settled on a recorded broadcast of Rachael Yamagata in concert at Sidney Harman Hall in Washington, DC showing on Amp Genie, cable station 837.

They were eating slices of fresh kiwi Dru had come by with earlier.

"Mr. Croker is dying," Dru had told them. "I'm not staying on, but I'll see things through until the estate is sold, including his funeral arrangements. His estranged daughter, Eleanor, hasn't been here in two decades, but she's the intended personal representative. What that means for you here, Allison, I can't say. Things could stay the same and you'll just pay her the rent. Or Eleanor could sell the place outright. I just wanted to give you a heads-up now."

"We could get a place together," Leah said after hearing that bombshell with Allison. "I haven't had a roomie since Kennesaw, but I'm outgrowing my one-bedroom job. Plus, I have no guy prospects. What the hey, right? It makes sense."

"It could work," Allison said, nowhere near as unruffled by the thought of moving in a hurry as she might've, if not for the glorious update on Amp Genie during a commercial break:

Not even a full week since his release from a Los Angeles prison, Brigadiers drummer, Jake McCray, first reported to be rejoining his bandmates for a new album and confirmed national tour, is quitting the band. Inside sources tell us McCray is committed to recording with The Brigadiers for their still-untitled ninth studio album, after which he is said to be stepping down. The band will feature former Rawk Skewl drummer, Billy Dozier for the upcoming 38 city reunion tour. The album marks the band's first in eleven years and The Brigadiers' first live tour in eight. No available comments have been made from McCray nor his bandmates.

The news report showed interchanging scenes of Jake McCray's younger days via slices cut from The Brigadiers' music videos, followed by a capture of his release from the Twin Towers Correctional Facility. His smug grin and faint wave to the cameras a week ago had set Allison off. This time, she put her own hand out to the television and waved at him back.

"Goodbye, asshole," she murmured as her eyes flooded then leaked.

"Take *that* you bastard," Leah gasped with an uneasy laugh. She latched her arms around Allison's shoulders and pulled her close, rocking her back and forth before kissing her friend upon a moist cheek. "You shook him up, though I still say you should rat his worthless ass out. Chasing him back underground would only be skimming the surface if it was me."

"I love you, Leah, but you're *not* me," Allison said. "I'm done with Jake McCray. I'm satisfied he knows I exist and just the idea of me showing up in his life is enough payback."

"I hope it haunts him to the grave."

"Yes, and I don't want to think about it anymore."

"Brighter Horizons will be sorry to lose you, Allison."

Allison gave Pam a firm nod before saying, "It's nothing personal. I need a reset. I'm moving in with a friend and, well, I'm sorry, is all I can say. Clarita's ready to take lead. I recommend you keep her in the twos. The kids love her. Hunter, especially, and we all know what a handful that one is."

Her soon-to-be-former boss smirked, but she looked dismayed, sick even.

"I appreciate the vote of confidence," Pam told Allison. "In all honesty,

I agree with you, though I was planning on moving Clarita to the fives. I was going to promote her to head teacher anyway."

"What about Meg?"

Pam glanced at the door to her office, making sure it was closed.

"You beat me to the punch, Allison. I'm also stepping down. Meg will be the new Director. She wanted it, she can have it."

"You sound bitter," Allison said, reaching across Pam's desk. The current director received Allison's hand with a one-time squeeze of shared understanding before she pulled hers away.

"Nah," Pam said with a passive heave. Her darting gaze around her office told a different story. "I'm glad for Meg, but if you think a two-year-old like Hunter's a handful, be glad you got your two weeks in. You'll beat me out of here by a day."

"What'll you do after you're gone?"

"Anything but day care. Todd and I are moving to the shore, Tybee Island. He has to relocate for his job, and I'm still sending out resumes. Pickings are kinda slim, but Todd's getting a sweet raise out of the deal. Helps digest this transition. It'll be tough for a while, but we'll make do. Like you, I'm looking forward to a reset."

"Wow," Allison said, shaking her head back and forth with a mixed bag of empathy and surprise. Part of her couldn't wait for her last two weeks to be over. Another part wanted to hug Pam with everything she had.

"You have a new job lined up, I take it."

"There's a day care in the office building where my friend works. No offense, they pay better."

"None taken," Pam said with a fuller laugh. "I'd do the same in your shoes. Tell me, something, though. You haven't been yourself lately. Is everything alright, or were you just nervous about your resignation?"

"Both," Allison said, shaking her head up and down this time. Relief more than anxiety coated her face and nudged her tightened shoulder to relax for the first time in a week.

Her stomach felt the best it had since Jake McCray got out of jail, and Allison was no longer locked up inside. She'd peed three times this morning after two cups of hazelnut coffee and the rest of Dru's kiwi for breakfast. Each time feeling more purged than the last. Leah had gone home last night, and Allison fell asleep within minutes after the two embraced over a long, triumphant cry filled with respite.

"You've been through something," Pam probed with a curious furrow of her eyebrow. "I can tell, woman-to-woman. Whatever it is, though, I think you've found your light at the end of the tunnel."

"I *made* my own light," Allison said, offering her hand out again to Pam as she stood up, this time for a handshake.

B.L.M.

"MAN, JUST STOP."

"What? We've been friends for ages, Marcus. Why can't I—"

"Because you *can't*, Sam."

The sun torched the city, carrying an ostensible intent to break wills with no apparent discrimination. The summer vapors pounded both ebony and pale skins alike with 96-degree fury, adding to the agitated swell already in the air. To both men approaching their fifties, the muggy air smelled and tasted of effluvium, a pungent tang of must, char, and rotten vegetables. Having retreated from a tear gas retort at the front line of a well-fortified demonstration, people said the heat felt like oppression.

A block away, a rasta-pocked swirl of reggae swirled like an urban prayer of dissent to Jah above the derelict row homes on Smallwood Street. Each wah-splashed guitar stroke and calypso-styled dub beat protesting a long-standing poverty. Jah people had lessened in numbers over the years in favor of a hipster army of neo rappers catching on with a new generation which flaunted the "n" word with even more flagrance than Ice-T and N.W.A. years ago. Richard Pryor long before them. Their lowbrow liturgy was spewed amidst a spindling drum machine you could hear in any corporate parking garage in Midtown as easily as any 'hood.

Shards of broken glass from smashed windows glistened on the asphalt like fading hope. Businesses around the block were boarded up against further looting, which had begun here the prior Thursday, fueled to full-on pillaging in the DuBois section a mere two blocks away. Only a week ago, people were getting their hair done, their groceries bought and rubbing elbows over beer and barbecue. The optimistic lure of smoked meat from Hip Hop Pit Beef had since been replaced by taint.

Only a week ago, people were picking up the city bus where a public bench had now been knocked over, the backrest slats defiled with the blue-sprayed edict, **"FUCK D12! FUCK THE POLICE! B.L.M."** Along the side of an old Buick which had been serviced an ignoble Molotov cocktail when the protests began, someone (perhaps the same would-be graffiti radical) had scrawled the edict, in the same primary color, **"REMEMBER RODNEY KING...FREDDIE GRAY...GEORGE FLOYD...B.L.M.!!!"**

On the blistering street, stomped and smudged amidst a rubble of rocks, bottle caps, cigarette butts, Big Mac containers, discarded latex gloves and medical face coverings was a handmade cardboard sign. Less than an hour ago, it had been held high in support of the forthcoming marchers. It bore the declaration, boldly impressed in black magic marker, **"EQUALITY IS LIFE...BIGOTRY IS DEATH."**

"I didn't think someone would actually swat it out of my hand like I have no right," Sam muttered, looking with caution at his friend, who was sieving water from a plastic bottle into each of his eyes.

A grubby film not only coated his faint skin which could've used a good tanning, it had turned Sam's sky-blue Banana Republic dress shirt to a visual representation of nausea. His wife, Nadine, had just bleached a spaghetti stain out of it last night. If she could see him now, Nadine would give him a tongue lashing to last long through the next bleaching and the one after that. Sam's tan cargo parts were on the verge of turning olive, making him regret coming to a protest march dressed for a political rally at a suburban sports bar.

Marcus squeezed his pupils and kept his sable head tilted backwards, letting the water flush into them. The carryover rivulets glistened inside his flourishing black mustache and beard which were betraying swells of gray pocks. Identical to his friend, Marcus had come to the march overdressed. His gray button-down shirt and khaki pants were both drenched in sweat and grit, sticking to his sizeable frame which he'd kept reasonably pared with dumbbell curls at home along with his evening walks. Marcus grunted at first from a carryover sting, then he let loose an audible sigh having nothing to do with relief.

"Whoever it was did you a favor," Marcus murmured, blinking a few times before dipping his head down. "The rubber bullets were flying faster than the canisters. I'm lucky I didn't get clipped. I saw a lot of banged up people. More blood than welts. People were screaming as if they'd been shot by real bullets."

"I know I'm not black," Sam beseeched, looking down at his crushed homemade sign and shaking his head. "Hell, I struggled with the entire idea of coming down here, the way things keep escalating."

"Well, I *am* black," Marcus said in a gruff tone. "The gas bath I just took says it's best you stay the hell out of this. It ain't your fight anyway."

"Maybe not," Sam said back, soft at first, but his pitch began to rise. "You're my friend, though. That's all the reason I need to—"

"I told you to stop this Freedom Fighter trip you're on, Sam. You don't belong in this. At our age, I'm a damned enough fool for getting involved myself, but it *is* the right thing."

"How can you say that to me, Marcus? Jesus, you're acting like I'm doing this as some sort of fad."

"Says the skeptic who argued with me a couple years ago Kaepernick was only doing the kneel to sell jerseys."

"Right, and look what it's become now. I *get* it, Marcus."

"What it's *become*," Marcus growled, squinting through his pain as the fluids leaked down both sides of his chiseled cheeks, "is bigger than you or me. Just because you can still recite old Rage Against the Machine lyrics and you wear a Curtis Mayfield shirt sometimes like you're some ageless proletariat insurgent don't make you one of us."

Now it was Sam's turn to sigh.

"Look, Marcus, we have a lot of miles between us, starting all the way back in college. We both did papers on Malcolm X for Sociology 101, remember that?"

"Yeah," Marcus answered, showing the first sign of a smile while swabbing his eyes with his shirt sleeve. "We were both on the hunt for *Malcolm X Talks to Young People* in the library. You got there first."

"You were kinda pissed at me, too, as I recall," Sam said, running a hand across his close-buzzed dome. "You sounded then like you do now. Like I was trespassing."

"Yeah," Marcus said again. "There was no tear gas or pepper spray then."

For the first time since the protest turned ugly, Sam laughed. It was hearty, robust, anticlimactic to the sweltering chaos which had been quelled by the city police only moments ago. To a few other stunned stragglers shambling into the block, Sam's laughter seemed out of place. In fact, their puzzled and incensed expressions forced Sam to compose himself. From across the street, he heard someone sneer, "Laugh it up, cracker, then get your white ass on outta here."

Despite his searing eyes, Marcus gestured toward the heavy man who'd shouted his derogatory dismissal, insinuating with a silent edict to Sam as if to claim, *Need I say more?* The man's left cheek was as swollen as his belly. The hole in his soggy jeans was stained crimson. He looked like he'd just gotten through a rumble.

"Yeah, I heard him, okay? You want me to go, I'll go, but hear me out a minute. Can you do you that much for an old friend?"

Marcus let his woozy nod serve as his response.

"We started off, not so much as adversaries, but competitors, maybe? Is that the right word?"

"Sounds about right," Marcus acquiesced. "Competitors for an A on the same paper with the same figurehead."

"You couldn't get your head around the fact I'd been inspired by Malcolm even before choosing him for my paper. I'd been studying him, the Panthers, Watts, the CORE, the SNCC, the Little Rock Nine..."

"Point taken, Sam."

"Then I evoke to you how we'd shared our research with each other. You were impressed by what I'd dug up and vice-versa. We swapped numbers. We agreed you would check out the Malcolm X book on your student I.D. You read it in two days before handing it over to me. On a leap of faith I would return it, someone you'd just met, since we sat far opposite of each other in the lecture hall. We collaborated, but we used our own voices and made sure we wrote different sequences. We both got A's on our papers. I've never made a friend quite the same way I did you, man."

"Yeah," Marcus said with a creak of a smile. "You were *alright*. It helped we both loved football, Shaft movies, and Caribbean jerk."

"Funkadelic, Clint Eastwood, Prince, pepper and onion sausages, tacos, baseball, the freaking Muppets. What's it going on now, Marcus, 28 years? I know we don't see each other but a few times a year for cookouts and Ravens games because of our schedules and families, but it was civil rights that first brought us together. If you stop and think about that a moment, then why *wouldn't* I be here, at this critical moment in history, to be there for you, brother?"

"You don't *have* to, is what I'm saying, *brother*."

"Don't mock me, Marcus. Please. Our wives would rail us both if they heard all of this stupid bickering."

"Trudy's gonna rail me anyway for being out here. She begged me not to come down. I gave her everything but an actual promise."

"If Nadine l knew I'd come down here, she'd..."

"She'd be right to, Sam!" Marcus interrupted. "It's not a white man's burden!"

"Are you even watching the news these days, Marcus? I'm hardly the only white guy coming out in the streets. White, black, Hispanic, Asian, Native American, male, female, LGBTQ... injustice is injustice, and enough is enough. Man, why am I having to tell *you* this, of all people? Did you even learn anything with me back in college?"

"Alright, Sam, alright. You want to stay and get your head beat in, be my guest."

"It's my choice if that happens, isn't it?" Sam asked lifting his hand up a moment with the intent to soothe his friend, but letting it drop back for the time being.

"One of the guys who fired the tear gas," Marcus said with less of a wince as the burn in his eyes began to ease. "Even through his face shield, I know I've seen him before, in front of the old courthouse. I remember the last name on his badge, Lambert. We were both getting a cheeseburger from this street vendor, Charlie Shreeve. Everyone calls him 'Ol Shreevy downtown."

"Shreevy sells the best damn burger in town," Sam said with a sharp nod. "Screw the chains."

"Officer Lambert let me in front of him in line, polite as all get-out. We even talked for a moment about Mustangs and Chargers since a few had rumbled by in the street. Nice guy, I thought. No racist cop there, so far as you'd be able to tell in a civilized setting. That was before today. I want to say the man's just doing his job, and I'd like to hope he was as scared of us as we were of him and his SWAT backup. I don't know, man. I can't pretend to know what it's like being a cop, but killing a man in the wide open, a brutal detention like Floyd got...Christ, Sam, the guy was crying for his mother..."

"We're *all* pissed, Marcus. That's what you need to understand. The whole scope of the problem is beyond black and white now."

"But it's a *black* people's problem."

"For which outsiders are taking an interest in helping to rectify. Strength in numbers is the only way change will ever come, you must know this. All these years, Marcus, I never realized you could be so stubborn."

Marcus remained quiet while Sam continued.

"I mean, what legacy did Malcolm X *really* leave for us? He broke off from the Nation, took his hajj and he found enlightenment in the motherland of Islam. You know where I'm going."

"You can probably quote him better than I can, since your meticulous brain is hard-wired like an encyclopedia."

"I don't need to tell *you* I'm getting older, so I'm not as meticulous as I used to be," Sam noted, letting his eyes flutter a moment in recollection. "I still read Malcolm's speeches a couple times a year, though. They energize me, man. Malcolm said, 'I tell sincere white people, 'Work in conjunction with us - each of us working among our own kind.' Let sincere white individuals find all other white people they can who feel as they do, and let them form their own all-white groups, to work trying to convert other white people who are thinking and acting so racist. Let sincere whites go and teach non-violence to white people! We will completely respect our white co-workers. They will deserve every credit. We will give them every credit. We will, meanwhile, be working among our own kind, in our own black communities, showing and teaching black men in ways that only other black men can—that the black man has got to help *himself*. Working separately, the sincere white people and sincere black people actually will be working together.'"

"The quote finishes with 'In our mutual sincerity, we might be able to show a road to the salvation of America's very soul.' I remember. That's how I ended my paper."

"I'm for truth, no matter who tells it," Sam said, opening his arms apart to his friend. "I'm for justice, no matter who it's for or against. In the end, it's about human rights, isn't it? Don't we *all* matter?"

Marcus received Sam in a tight hug filled with loud claps upon their respective backs. More people entered the block and over his friend's shoulder, Sam saw a few heads bob approvingly in their direction.

"Sorry they dissed your sign," Marcus said after they let go of one another. He reached down into the street to retrieve it. "I wasn't seeing straight to get the message, but people *should* see this."

"That means a lot, Marcus," Sam said. "You alright, though? Your eyes look like the maroon side of a Rubik's Cube."

"They hurt like hell, but my heart hurts worse. This isn't going to be a quick fix, any of it."

"No, it isn't," Sam affirmed, squeezing Marcus' shoulder. "You and I are a little long in the tooth for this, but we can't let the youngbloods shoulder it all. First time I've had genuine optimism for them. I'm trying to get my head around our parents doing this same thing right before *we* were born."

"Heavy stuff," Marcus said, handing over the battered cardboard over to Sam. "Get your sign up and let's take another lap. We'll see who follows."

"Right on," Sam said, holding his sign above his head as the two stepped into the street, rallying for change louder than the clapping reggae down the street.

Coming of Rage

1982.

"WANT A HOT DOG?" Gloria asks me. "It's all I know how to make. Aside from Pop Tarts and cinnamon toast, but *anyone* can do that."

I'm hungry because I haven't eaten anything yet today. Mom even left the box of Apple Jacks on the table for me this morning. Next to my favorite *Empire Strikes Back* bowl I just can't get rid of, along with the matching plastic mug with Luke, Han, and Leia's heroic smiles around it. They can make wisecracks in the face of death. They've won a lot of battles, but Han going into carbon freeze and Luke being told he's Darth Vader's kid after getting his hand lopped off by the same dad, of all things...where are the jokes then, except with your action figures, where you get to make a better ending? In my world, Boba Fett gets drop-kicked by Chewie into a trash compactor and Yoda saves Luke by cramming Vader's scary helmet straight up his Sith derriere. Leia and Han fly off in the Millennium Falcon to a beach planet where they have Solo-Organa triplets.

You get rid of your toys and kid things by now, so the rest of the boys my age in the neighborhood say. They smoke cigarettes and pot and they steal beers from their dads. They tell dirty jokes and create their weekly "Top 5" lists of the girls from school whom they most want to see naked. They also brag they've all *done it,* but I'm not sure if I believe any of them. They're jerks, anyway.

I don't do the drugs and I haven't seen a girl naked, much less done it.

I'm so un-cool I've become the only one listed as a Top 5 Loser in our development. I cried in the theater at the end of *E.T.,* so I guess the other kids are right.

I like to shoot hoops, but my jump shots suck worse than Brainy Smurf's leadership skills. My lay-ups are more like a lay-down-and-die. My dribbling, pathetic. I make a lot of racket thumping a basketball and I tend to launch it over my head. When I'm by myself on the court, that's not really a problem, other than worrying half the neighborhood's watching me make an idiot of myself, since the court is smack in the middle of things. You're on display for the whole section, good or bad. It's why I'm usually indoors.

When I do sneak onto the court, the other neighborhood guys dart in and take my ball from me. They always smell like tobacco or Budweiser, and I wonder why their parents haven't figured it out and grounded them for life. Instead, they show up, never one at a time. It's always as a group. A gang. As if I'm somebody they need to stack numbers against. I'm ashamed to say I sit to the side and wait for them to be done, because my dad will torch my butt if I let anyone steal my stuff.

All these things make people call me a queer around here.

No one's heard me say I've had a crazy crush on Catherine Bach going on three years now, though I've been vocal enough. Barbara Eden, Julie Newmar, and Yvonne Craig before her. I couldn't have been louder telling the other guys these things. As if they care, and I mean, who doesn't like Catherine Bach? *Dukes of Hazzard* is getting boring, but Daisy's still the reason to watch.

I don't really have anything against guys who like other guys and girls who like other girls. Not really, but when you're not a queer and get called one anyway…it sucks worse than the Atari version of *Pac-Man.*

I've had dreams about Catherine Bach, you know, *that* kind. The first time I had a wet dream with my pajama bottoms soaked and sticky, I'd been scared to death. Like Carrie White when she'd gotten her period for the first time but hadn't been told what it was by her Jesus freak mother.

Which brings me to Gloria, and her hot dogs and MTV on a rainy August Thursday.

Summer vacation hasn't been much to fill the essay I know is coming once seventh grade starts next month. Stupidest theme ever, "My Summer Vacation." Not all of us go to Disney World or the Grand Canyon. My parents took me to Hershey Park for a day in June and that was gnarly, even having to wait forty minutes to ride the Sooper Dooper Looper. Seeing *Firefox* and *Tron* back-to-back with Dad and Uncle Larry on the same day in July, totally awesome. A couple of Orioles games they won, but otherwise, a flusher of a summer.

At least I've had Gloria.

Gloria's my friend and, well, I have a crush on her. Yeah, I've had *those* kinds of dreams about Gloria, but no way would I ever tell her that. She'd end our friendship, or worse, kick me in the nuts before kicking me out the door.

I can hear the boiling water from the kitchen overtop Duran Duran's "Hungry Like the Wolf" video on the tv in Gloria's living room. I can smell those heated meat tubes (what my Dad calls hot dogs) and I can picture them flopping around in a bubbling bounce inside the pot. Easy-peasy to make, as Gloria says. I could do hot dogs if my parents would just allow me to use the daggone stove.

I'm jealous Gloria, same age as me, is trusted to use the stove with nobody but her and her older brother, Mike, at home during the day. Of course, Mike is always out the door around 8:00 a.m. and he comes home right before dinner. I've asked Gloria where he goes during the day, but she has no idea.

Fine by me, since Mike's been known to beat the crap out of guys who've tried to hit on Gloria. I'm the only guy he allows into the house with his sister and it's only because he's heard all the other guys call me a queer. I'm glad he has no clue about the dreams I have about her.

"Sure," I tell Gloria, and though I'm ready to eat, I'm also ready to barf. I'm nervous right now, like I get when I sneak downstairs in the middle of the night and put cable tv on to watch gory horror movies my parents forbid me from watching, like *The Thing* and *Visiting Hours*. They're gonna catch me sometime but I can't help myself. *The Boogens* is on at 1:30 a.m. tonight and I promise you I'll be there, my face close to the television on low volume so nobody hears me. If I can force myself not to eat those crunchy bacon-flavored Cheetos, I'll get away with it.

"Have you seen the new Prince video yet?" Gloria asks me, and I can't help but watch the wiggle of her butt, since it's obvious she's wearing no underwear beneath her green gym shorts. "You know, 'Little Red Corvette?'"

"Yeah," I tell her shadow once she turns into the kitchen. On MTV, Duran Duran changes to Tom Petty and The Heartbreakers' "You Got Lucky" video. I smile and tell myself, *You wish, Ben.*

"What do you think Prince is singing about?" she calls out from the kitchen. I hear Gloria turn the pot off and the gurgling noise simmers down. Afterwards, there's the sound of an opening and closing drawer, then a cabinet door smacking another one, followed by the tinkling pull down of ceramic plates. Gloria's family has the same plate set we do, the one with the blue-green floral pattern around the edges. You can get them at Safeway with bonus coupons, depending on how much you spend.

"Driving fast, I guess," I answer Gloria. "When we get old enough to drive, I want a Trans-Am Firebird, black, like in *Smokey and the Bandit*. I'm such a spaz."

"Nah," Gloria replies. "Mike's getting his license next year and he's saving up for an actual Corvette. I'm getting the Mongoose BMX bike he rides now when that happens, I can't wait. You want mustard or ketchup?"

"Mustard."

"Cool," she tells me. "I knew I liked you for a reason, Ben."

Gloria comes back and hands me a plate holding a mustard covered hot dog. Esskay brand, like you get at Memorial Stadium for Orioles games. I saw my favorite player, Eddie Murray, smack a dinger against the California Angels when Dad took me to a game last Saturday. It was amazing, especially when the stadium rang with Earth, Wind and Fire's "September" after the field cleared; as in we have high hopes the O's will make the playoffs this year. I had a hot dog just like this one, and Dad and I split a bag of salted peanuts. It's those days I'm not so afraid of my father, except when it gets to last call in the eighth inning and he's barking at the beer vendor to hurry up and get to us.

"Thanks," I say, and the aroma of the hot dog makes me feel, not so much sick anymore, like I haven't eaten in days. I take a huge bite and look at Gloria to make sure she doesn't think I'm actually *being* a spaz. She's in mid-twirl sitting down with her plate, but instead of inside the love seat across the room as she was earlier, she's now planted next to me. Her being this close, I just now smell her perfume. I don't know anything about perfumes, other than Mom uses Jean Nate after a shower and she loves Evening in Paris. So does Dad, of course.

Gloria smells like honeysuckle, like the farm behind our old house in Woodbine, about a million miles away from this awful suburb in Perry Hall. I miss my old friends Chris, Danny, and Steven. They never tried to steal my basketball. They didn't smoke. They didn't call me a queer.

"You know what I think Prince means?" Gloria asks, taking a smaller bite of her hot dog than I did. Hers is more of a nibble, so she can speak again right away. "I think he's talking about a woman's private part, you know, *down there.*"

"What?" I holler out, nearly choking on my next bite. I try not to laugh out of fear Gloria will get mad at me, but this is the first time she's talked about anything sexual to me. It's weird, like talking about baseball or horror movies or G.I. Joe with her. Still, I'm kind of happy about it, just the same.

"I'm serious, Ben," she says, placing her hand on my knee for a just a moment before pulling it away. My body lights up like it never has before. I've been touched by a girl, and I'm not talking about my older cousins. Not even the silly girls in their violet and yellow barrettes who chased me around in second grade, kissing up and down my arm and going "muah muah muah" like Pepe Le Pew once they caught me. My legs feel on fire, like I've just run twenty laps around the entire development.

"I guess, maybe," I blurt out, trying to think the same way as Gloria, but I've got the clapping groove of Prince's song in my head, not the words, really digging the way the drum machine and synthesizers hit that shuffle-slide nobody else can do. So cool.

"You're a guy, so you wouldn't know how a woman's body works," Gloria says with a shrug before taking a bigger bite and swallowing the wad quicker than I would've expected. "No offense, Ben."

"They taught us some of that stuff in Science class," I say, though it's for nothing, since Gloria's focused on the television.

I finish my hot dog as MTV VJ Nina Blackwood chatters about an upcoming world premiere of Devo's "Whip It" before a woman with even more shocked hair than Nina's comes on. Dale Bozzio of Missing Persons, looking like she dipped the right side of her head into blue and pink paint containers, swaying in a leather gladiator outfit and looking like she could kick everyone's tails, even with that goofy squeak she tosses at the end of some of the verse lines.

"Do you hearrrr meeeee," Gloria sings along. "Do youuuuu carrrrre...oh, Ben, I love this song!"

I do too, though I sing worse than my grandfather, who was probably not too bad when he was younger. When he tries now, it takes all we have as a family not to humiliate him during his zombie groans.

It's one of the best days I've had this lousy summer, even with crappy weather outside. Only hiking by myself at the nearby quarry, MTV, and Orioles games gives me any real happiness. And Gloria, of course.

That's when the knock comes at the door.

At first, it's a normal rap, like a rhythm as we were taught on those dumb blue sticks in Music class back in elementary. Then it gets louder, and more than one fist is doing the knocking. I hear the annoying chuckles along with the rising bangs and I know this day of awesomeness is heading south.

"Alright, already!" Gloria snaps as she gets up from the couch. I want to tell her to just ignore it all, since I know who's on the other side.

I shouldn't be surprised, because everyone likes Gloria, especially her cute freckles that stretch from cheek-to-cheek and her feathery red hair, and a body that no 12-year-old should own. I hear the guys all say Gloria could pass for 15 or 16, and that's why Mike is so protective of his sister. It's even been said he once tried to get it on with her, though no one's had the guts to make the accusation to his face.

"What's up, Gloria?" I hear Kyle Hanley shout as soon as she opens the door. He sounds like a menace, and he *is* one. He's dropped acid a few times, once in plain sight on the basketball court. He turned into a lunatic that day, the first time he'd called me a queer in front of everyone. He not only took my basketball that day, he launched it down the slope. It dented Mrs. Metcalf's Datsun, for which *I* got blamed. Dad refused to pay for the damage and instead, he had a good row with Kyle's dad over it. Kyle fessed up, but in the end, nobody paid for Mrs. Metcalf's ding. It's still there.

"Hi, Kyle," Gloria responds in a sweet tone that makes my chewed up hot dog pieces sink like rock chunks. It's as if she *likes* the jerk.

"What're you and the queer up to?" Kyle asks in a bossy manner, and I can see him pushing his head over her shoulder. I also see Johnny Conway, Elvin Sizemore and Ricky Pingel hovering outside. "We know he's here with you. Hey, queer, I see you! I'd ask what you're doing with Gloria, but the answer is nothing! You're queer!"

The laugher outside makes me angry, and I feel my fists ball up. I want to hit them. Every day I see them, I want to hit them. When they steal my ball, I want to hit them. Every time they call me *that*, I want to hit them.

Kyle nudges Gloria out of the way and the other boys follow him in.

"Thanks for the invite!" Ricky jokes, and they all sound like tickled hyenas. I want to hit them even more.

"Guys, you can't..." Gloria protests, but she's already shut the front door, like she's given up and worse, like she's happy to have so much company. I don't understand any of it.

"What's shakin' bacon?" Elvin snorts to Gloria, and worse, he smacks her on the butt in passing. To my disbelief, Gloria not only lets him get away with it, she giggles at the whole thing. I'd have thought she'd slap him a good one for that.

"Hiya, queer," Kyle says to me as he gets closer. I catch him looking down at my fists and I can see it in his eyes; he wants to see how far he can push me before I'll swing.

"Ease up, there, killer," Johnny cracks at me, punching me on the arm before flopping down on the sofa. "What's for lunch, Gloria? You save any for us?"

"When's Mike getting home?" Elvin asks Gloria.

"Dinner time, maybe later, who knows? I don't keep tabs."

"Peace, dude," Kyle cracks at me, pulling out a rolled joint from his pocket and waving it in my face, like he's trying to tempt me. All I can think of is Dad tearing layers off my skin if that thing gets within an inch of my lips. "We're just here to hang, alright?"

"You can't smoke that in here, Kyle!" Gloria shouts. "My parents grounded Mike a whole week when they caught him doing weed in his room."

"Oooohhhh, a whole week," Johnny groans like he's the funniest kid in the neighborhood. No, the planet. His buddies laugh as if it's true.

"I'm serious, Kyle! Don't do it!"

"Yeah, Kyle," I say, standing up to him for the first time. "Go do it in your own house."

"Whoa!" Kyle yells, and I brace myself to be socked in the face. That never comes. "Look who has his balls all a sudden!"

"Didn't know you had it in you, queer!" Elvin mocks me. More of that dumb laughter which makes me even madder.

"Maybe he's not so queer after all!" Kyle blares at me. "What've you two been doing, anyway? Are we interrupting something? Something Mike would want to know about?"

"Oh, shut up," Gloria says in a tough girl voice, what I'd expected and hoped for when Elvin had cracked her rear end. "There's nothing going on between us. Gimme a break."

"Oh, really?" Kyle says and like that, he has Gloria by the arm.

"Hey! What are you doing, Kyle?" she bellows at him, but I see something I wish I hadn't. Gloria's not only faking it all, she's smiling.

Two sets of hands grab both of my arms and I'm struggling to keep my feet on the floor. We're all about the same height. How Elvin and Ricky are so brawny, I don't know, but they have me across the living room faster than if I'd run on my own.

Kyle yanks open the door to the half bathroom on the main level and he shoves Gloria inside. For all the times I've been hanging with Gloria this summer, I've never had to go to the bathroom, which is normally kept closed. The bright pink paint inside of the half bath tingles my eyes a moment.

"Show us what you're made of, queer!" Elvin yells into my ear and it hurts, as if someone's just blown a saxophone right next to my face.

I feel myself stumble into the bathroom and Gloria catches me from falling the short distance into the towel rack before the door slams like being trapped inside a haunted house and the lights go out.

I can feel her chest smashed against me as I try to stand straight in the dark. The short time we're not touching each other, I feel Gloria's hand pat my side a bunch of times until she has my hand.

Outside, I hear the guys telling me to put it inside of Gloria and all the filthiest language you can imagine. They're drowned out by the new sound of the overhead fan, then the hiss of running water. Gloria must have a cat's vision, she flips it all on so fast. She still has hold of my hand when I hear, even with all the commotion in the darkness, what sounds like something unfastening.

I don't feel Gloria tugging my hand to it, but I do feel every bit of spongy flesh, part of it hardening between my trembling fingers. She's mashing my hand against one of her breasts, while patting at my hip, searching her way between my legs.

This is the moment I've dreamt about with Gloria, yet I don't feel anything down there right now. I feel paralyzed, like my legs won't work, much less *that*. I'm scared and it gets worse once the guys start beating on the door outside.

"You going to *do* anything?" I hear from Gloria, but it's not the gentle and kind friend's voice I've grown used to this summer. Now she sounds mad at me, and it just makes the whole thing worse. This isn't how I'd hoped my first sexual encounter would go. It feels more like rape. Who's raping who in this case, though? You never hear of *girls* raping a *guy*.

Once Gloria's found my privates through my jeans, she sighs at me since nothing's happening. All I'm thinking of in that second is Mike ripping the door off its hinges and breaking my hand before ripping the rest of me apart.

"How ya doin' in there, queer?" Kyle yells, sounding like his mouth's right against the door.

"I'm done with this," Gloria snarls, swatting my hand away and I can tell she's trying to put herself back together after bumping into me a few times. I hear the water shut off before the fan, then I hear the jackhammer of my nervous heart inside my eardrums. It's squishy sounding.

I get a final whiff of Gloria's honey scent before she rumbles at me, "Disappointing."

Even though the guys have been blocking the bathroom door, Gloria's good and mad. She shoves the door open hard enough to scatter them.

"Geez, that was quick," Johnny teases her.

I feel him calling me the word I hate more than any other in the entire dictionary before Kyle says it for the umpteenth time.

"What, she too much for you, queer?" he heckles me.

That's all it takes. The fear goes away along with the embarrassment. I don't know who I despise more between the five them, the guys or Gloria. At least the guys are predictable. I never once thought Gloria could be like this. I know I'll never set foot in this house again, and I'll resent Gloria more than appreciate her for giving me my first ever grab beneath the clothes.

"Call me that again," I say through my teeth, fishing for anything else good to drum up. Something not just to come off as cool, but something they'll all remember. Something that'll get them off my case for good.

"Or you'll what?" Elvin blares, shoving past his friends to get in my face.

"I don't care what happens to me anymore," I say, taking a step out of the bathroom and meeting Elvin, almost nose-to-nose. "You won't know who I go after first, but I'll take you all down."

"What'd you say, punk?" Elvin asks, but I can tell I've gotten to him. He's nowhere near as loud. It's all the momentum I need. If I had the muscles to back up my mouth, it'd be over in seconds.

"I won't stop, so you'd better kill me first."

"Tough talk, jackoff," Elvin presses me. "Can you back it up?"

"Try me," I growl though my teeth. My head explodes on both sides from a rush of excitement, and I can feel everything I want from those two words. I may have to fight, and I want to now, whether I win or lose. Funny though, I don't think I'll have to.

"Ben! Jet back, dude!" Kyle shouts. It sounds strange, him calling me by my proper name, and not that word I hate so much.

"Everyone get out," Gloria orders us all, but it's me she's looking at, and I can see she's now very much afraid of me. "You, especially, psycho. I thought you were alright."

"You, Gloria," I say, making sure they all can hear me. "*You're* the one who's disappointing."

"Get bent," she says with the strongest voice she can dig up, but we all hear how terrified she sounds. Terrified but still mad. The others look at her as if she has snakes coming out her of her eyes.

As the guys get out of my way and I leave Gloria's house, it feels more of a loss than a win. Stepping into the rain, which has slowed up since I first got here, the cool wetness feels great upon my face, my ears, my arms. I hadn't realized how hot my skin had been.

I trudge up the hill, feeling like Carrie White at the tail end of her revenge for the pig's blood prank. I feel betrayed and I want to lash out. Gloria was my only friend in this neighborhood. For a while, I was special in her life, and now at the end of it all, I'm no better off than when we'd first moved to Perry Hall. I wish I had as much courage as I do right now to tell my parents I wish we never had.

My stomach hurts again and I try to take my mind off remembering what it had felt like touching Gloria. Only thing is, the more I think about her breast in my hand, the worse I feel.

Mom and Dad won't be home from work for another three hours. I know when I get inside, I'm going to put MTV on and hope they play Iron Maiden's "Flight of Icarus." I've never heard music like that before. Loud, *angry,* like I feel right now. I want to fly, on my way, like an eagle, to touch the sun. Only thing is, I'm not going to come crashing back down like Icarus. I'll fly, by God.

As I unlock the door to our house, I glance down the slope at Gloria's house. I know the guys are still in there, and for the first time since being on the couch with Gloria, I smile. I start laughing, in fact.

I see Mike gliding to the house on his Mongoose, back home early for a change.

It feels like a joke only I know the punch line to. It happens the way I hope it does. Mike hops off and lets his bike drift empty as it collapses to the sidewalk with a clatter in front of his and Gloria's house.

It doesn't take long, and I wish I had a camera to catch four boys racing out of that house as if Michael *Myers* had come crashing in there. If I'd startled them earlier, now they look like death was really coming for them. Yeah, Dr. Loomis, that *is* the boogeyman.

Anybody who's outside can watch it unfold, but I'm sure I'm the only one in the whole neighborhood cracking up to see Mike chasing after those jerks.

When I get inside my house and flip on the tube, it's like God himself is watching over me.

Iron Maiden is on MTV, flying as high as the sun...

In Search of Dave the Wave

THE STEAM FROM THE HEAT press hisses and caresses my chest, my favorite part to the process of t-shirt making. I know it sounds crazy, but after 31 years doing it, I still enjoy this. It's like bonding with the elements, even if the reaction is manmade. I love the sound of it, like controlled aggression. Even the smell of the vinyl decal pressing into cotton, it's something few take pleasure in. For me, it's the fragrance of freedom.

"How's this look?" I ask my current customer. He's a shaggy good ol' boy; his Confederate belt buckle pushes against his bloated nether region, swollen by a strict 12-ounce curl regimen. I can tell by the fading tattoo on his forearm his favorite beer is, and always has been, Schaefer. A closer look at his overcooked arms betrays white flecks amidst the crimson burn, a sign of melanoma he may not be aware of, much less care. He earns his bread and his Schaefers outdoors. On a road crew, perhaps.

I'm not trying to look, I swear, but I can tell a guy who's hornier for his gun than his wife next to him, a puffy, Schaefer-in-arms good ol' gal. She's flicking the spark wheel to her metallic lighter that has, you guessed it, the Schaefer brand embossed on the fluid carrier. The flame goes up then out with each stroke.

"There's no smoking in the store, ma'am," I say, feeling a smidge edgy Lady Firebug might have arson on the brain since there's no cigarette within sight. I'm hoping to bag this transaction before she torches the stack of water taffy next to her.

"I know it," she says with such impunity she's drawn not only the attention but the adoration of her husband. I could've been wrong about that gun, after all.

"Go on and put that away, Ellie," he tells her. "You're making this gentleman all nervous 'n such."

"His problem, not mine," Lady Firebug says without looking at me. I try not to roll my eyes up at her. The lighter goes into a faded, beat-up leather purse hanging from her bulbous neck and resting somewhere between her daunting bosom and chubby waist. On her body, it looks more like a harness.

Their filmy, scraggly hair could've been assembled with a stolen fork from an all-you-can-eat instead of an actual comb. They both smell like cheap suntan oil to go with their cheap sunglasses and the cheap Schaefer beer they'd had before coming into my shop. It's on their breaths and I'm close to puking thinking of these two swapping spit with that pale lager crap lingering on their hayseed breaths.

I've seen so many people over three decades running Wave Runner Tees & Souvenirs I've begun a silent hobby of profiling. I figure these crackers went to a big breakfast this morning because they're my only current customers at 2:32 p.m., a slower part on a summer's weekday for boardwalk entrepreneurs not peddling fries, lemonade, or icy drinks.

I then detect regurgitated sausage and I never touch the stuff. Which one of them tore ass in my store, I don't know, but uncouth is uncouth, no matter what redneck bunghole it ripped from.

They'd had long siestas in aluminum foldout chairs. He got in the water. She didn't, except maybe to her ankles. They're both as red as the logo for their favorite beer, except she's cooked down to said ankles, those being whiter than her bumpkin self. I pity her the more weight she gains, since those ankles look ready to give soon. Cased inside her flimsy flip flops, I wouldn't be surprised if she catches a rut between the slats of the boardwalk and crashes in epic fashion. They're both tough cusses, though, because they haven't complained one iota, except for the music pumping in my store. The Replacements, for the record.

"Right as rain," the guy says, tilting his shades down to see the printed 3X black shirt I've unfurled. As I predicted he would after wandering into my store, he chose one of the Second Amendment defense decals I offer. Hick couture depicting a double barrel shotgun and the call-to-arms emblem **"GIVE ME LIBERTY, GIVE ME MY RIGHTS TO DEFEND MYSELF...PROTECT THE 2**ND**"**

I nod and show the shirt to his wife.

"Whatchoo think, honey?" he asks her.

She snorts and nods before saying, "Love the shirt, but ain't too keen on this fairy music."

Anyone taking a shit on The Replacements can get the hell out of my store as a rule, but in this case, I have a t-shirt to sell. I ignore her and make a show of folding the shirt with care in mid-air, leaving the newly applied decal facing up and out. Tourists love such attention to detail, as if they never get it wherever they call home.

I can't hardly wait for these NRA poster children to pay and move on to the nearest Cabela's. Even though that chain fishing emporium would make a killing in a nautical burg like Ocean City, the closest one's three counties away. They sell guns there, too, right as rain.

"Ain't no Skynyrd," Sir Schaefer-a-Lot tells me as a gentle reprimand, as if by my switching to the local classic rock station, WBBE, my cred would soar in his eyes. "At least this store's run by *Americans*."

"Hell yeah to that," Lady Firebug says, putting up a flabby fist for her flabby husband to bop. He does, and I try not to laugh at their shimmying fat rolls.

"Give it another couple summers, though, the commies and towel heads'll take over the whole damn boardwalk. At least they got money, unlike the Mexicans. That'll do 'er, bud, what I owe ya?"

We square up to the tune of $15.89, including the six percent sales tax stroked to the Comptroller of Maryland. I watch them waddle their way out toward the inlet attractions and later, I figure, a seafood smorgasbord timed ahead of the vacationer rush to scarf the prime selections. I hope the guys on the OC Hammerhead took in a big haul this morning.

"Take 'er easy," Sir-Schaefer-a-Lot says, squashing the fold of the plastic bag as far down to its contents as he can cram inside his fist.

"Do the same," I respond, not bothering to address Lady Firebug. Yeah, calling the tunes I listen to in the store 'fairy music' gets you on my bad side worse than flicking a Bic like a nervous tic.

Keeping true to this summer's trend, political iron-ons have been the rage. You never know each season what's going to hit with the public. I've been down at the beach long enough to see the end of "the original party animal," Spuds Mackenzie's reign over the resort. When I dropped anchor here at Wave Runner Tees & Souvenirs, you couldn't give those tank tops away with Bud Light's former bull terrier pitch-dog hanging ten on the front.

Decals featuring sports, muscle cars, alcohol, sex, the military, weapons, gym rats, superheroes, tatted-up Disney princesses, ethnic superbia, MAGA, gay pride, and anything with a pot slogan lure people in here. **"KEEP ONE ROLLED"** and **"THIS GUY NEEDS A BEER"** with the upraised thumb jerks to the wearer are what I call my 'ol reliables. I sell those faithfully each year, along with **"BEACH PATROL"** hoodies and long sleeves amped by Johnny Cash tossing the finger.

Look, I'm a pragmatist and I have no political affiliation. My philosophy is Democrat bucks spend just as easily as Republican and both are bursting with a "team" mentality to blast their political principles at one another using their engorged chests. Reminds me of football season, when Ravens, Steelers, Redskins, Cowboys, Eagles and Giants fans talk smack to each other in my store as I steam press their team logos to whatever they pay me for. The superiority complex to it all cracks me up. Dr. Seuss was a damn prophet writing *The Sneetches*.

I'm an easygoing guy, a lenient boss, and even though I hear the heat press and whatever tunes I pump over the store intercom more than I do the ocean, it's been a kicked-back lifestyle long suitable to me. It's been a great people-watching hub and Lord, have I seen my share of characters.

Most are harmless; many drop money on things they'll never use outside of a beach vacation, which suits me just fine, so long as their card swipes clear my terminal. Some stoners disguised as surfers come into my store higher than the flapping trilobites at Kite Loft a couple blocks over. They don't qualify for legalized medicinal herb, so they still go by the street method—grass roots, if you will. They think because I'm a lifer I know connections. I do, but not *those* kinds of connections.

I hold the fort in my store from opening at 10:00 a.m. until this season's part-timers, Rachel and Andrew relieve me long enough to eat dinner and catch up my DVR a little before I come back at close to reconcile and shut down. I'm a twelve-hour operation, but that doesn't stop the last minute horndog from dashing in, buzzed and spry with an eye set on a clever decal blustering his monster dick size.

This is Rachel's second summer with me, and I can depend on her. There was a time I'd never put a face in the public forum which sported a hoop-punctured nostril and a bar in the brow. Times change, though, and unlike Andrew, Rachel's only called out sick one time since I hired her. Andrew's already been out four times in his first year with me and it's only the middle of July.

I idle toward the front of the store to see how much action is outside right now, and to catch a whisper of the tide. The squeaking seagulls get to my ears first, and their joyous chatter having scored castaway Thrashers french fries makes me smile, even if I know the dirty birds (as the locals call them) will be goners the more they eat that oily stuff.

Sir-Schaefer-a-Lot has a point in the fact the retail dynamic of Ocean City's boardwalk *has* changed, though he's hardly enlightened enough to know the outcropping of store proprietors and servers are an influx from Ukraine, not their Russian invaders. Many of my competing t-shirt shops were once owned by retiring or outright elderly folks having lost their taste for business. These were snapped up by newcomer Ukrainians and I know for some, this is just a pit stop to build enough capital toward a deeper trek into their adopted American homeland.

Thus far, the new ownership has collectively been nothing but polite, if reserved. They all seem focused, even in the quieter parts of the day. I wouldn't call them intense, but they have a keen eye on their environment, which includes their haughty American neighbors. If they're aware of the ethnocentricity swirling around them, they don't show it. The world has gone pro-Ukraine, at least, and they've seen far worse hatred at the doorstep to their homeland. The war-transplanted Ukrainian immigrants work hard, and they play a fair hand. Thus far, none of them have tried to undercut me except for a few cents now and then. I admire their quick grasp of American economics and hell, there's plenty enough to go around, especially on summertime weekends.

"Pryvit, Mark!"

Speaking of which, that would be my Ukrainian friend, Katya

Yurkovich.

Twenty-four, long-legged, calves toned by constant brisk walking. Thighs not so much thick but robust, they rise to support glutes which snag the attention of most of the male species who come across her. She floats more snow in her hair than we tend to get at the ocean during winter's peak. A personality as bright as an early June sunrise over the coastal horizon. A resistant smile Putin couldn't wipe away with his violent coup. An aspirant model, Katya is energy on two feet and the sweetest kid I've ever met.

"Whattya say, Donetsk?" I chirp at her, trying to be cooler than I really am. For Katya, it works, since Donetsk celebrates her home, the town she came from before the cannonade arrived.

I first met Katya, not her at her family's soft pretzel shop on 4th Street, but the popular beach bar, Seafarer's. This was in early May, the priming of tourist season which hits full bloom on Memorial weekend. Summers are made at Seafarer's if you're young. I know quite a few locals other than myself who haunt the joint in the off-season months, then disappear until November. It so happened I wanted a rum runner and Seafarer's unbeatable crab pretzel the night I ran into Katya, who pulled up a stool and a screwdriver on the rocks next to me. Her staying power at 126 pounds made us friends.

Youngbloods usually never have anything to do with me unless they have a job application in their hands, yet Katya had no problem keeping a conversation going. Even through her choppy English (better than most drunken college slobs around 11:30 every night) she'd talked to me clear past midnight about Donetsk, the Crimean and Carpathian Mountains which Katya had loved to ski at, and the most vital element to her being in the United States, her modeling drive. The Yurkovich family, like most of the others converging to Ocean City by way of Boston, flocked here due to poor economics and a rekindled war with a would-be Soviet reboot. The Crimean annexation came long before that.

"For you, my friend," Katya says, handing me a soft pretzel with a side container of cheese whiz. Since our screwdriver and rum runner summit at Seafarer's, Katya makes it a point to come my store once, sometimes twice a day. Most of the time, it's just to say hello and to shoot the breeze. Our convos always end with her trumpeting from a far stretch down the Atlantic, "I'm coming, New York!"

"Your old man's gonna think we're up to something if you keep bringing me freebies, Katya," I tell her, giving instead of receiving our now-customary hug.

"It's my business, no?" she flirts, firing me a wink. She does that a lot, but it never means anything, nor should it. She's had her eye on some strapping guy her age shuttling kids on and off slow-rolling mounted scooters and pole jumping ligneous animals down at the Trimper Rides. All going round and round in monotony. "Not to worry. Father knows about pretzels. Says good business relations amongst neighbors. How we did things in Ukraine."

"He's a good man. Give him my thanks, and these...hold up."

I whirl and jog to the center of the store to one of the knickknack tables I have stocked with coffee mugs, wooden plaques and shot glasses, all emblazoned with the resort name on them. I fish out five blue rimmed shot glasses with a dolphin bursting out of the tide and "Ocean City" scrawled in cursive across the top.

"I know you and your family are big drinkers," I tell her, handing over the shot glasses. They clink in the transfer to her extended fingers.

"Duzhe d'akuju, Mark," she chirps, throwing one long-limbed arm around me and giving me a return hug. I know by now her Ukrainian phraseology translates to thank you very, very much.

"Anytime," I answer her. So beautiful is her smile and her eyes determined to conquer more than a touristy beach town, I wish she were my own daughter so I could root her on as more than just a friend.

"I see you soon," Katya tells me as she detaches and cuts the air in half with a lurching backwards step. "I'm *coming*, New York!"

"I sure hope so," I tell her, taking a bite of the pretzel to show my gratitude. If the legs stretching from her hip-hugging white cargo shorts aren't Manhattan-worthy, I don't know what are.

I watch Katya bound down the boardwalk like she's already set foot out of the Port Authority with the afterglow of Midtown summoning her like a beacon. I chuckle as one of the younger vacationer males gets a sour look from his flustered girlfriend. She snaps her hand free of his in response to the way his head twirls after Katya. Before Katya vanishes, I detect a couple of old Bingo biddies sneer to her shadow, their jealousy ringing louder than the four beat and cowbell clang of "Alex Chilton" over my head.

Half-dancing my way to the register with my late afternoon snack courtesy of Katya, I nod to a newcomer family who've slipped in from the opposite corner opening.

"How're you doing, folks?" I ask, feeling chipper. A standard line I've uttered a gazillion times by now, but I embrace the warmth in my voice. No robotic drone or plain civility this time. I'm in a good mood. Riding the wave, as it were. "Anything I can do for you, just holler."

"Thank you," the mother responds loud enough to cut through The Replacements without wrecking the pulse, which impresses me.

She twiddles her fingers, but she's looking in the direction of a boy I'd peg to be about nine. His sister's older and carries a swagger. I'd put the sibling at 13. The brother idolizes her, since he won't stay out of her vicinity. I can tell the sister is exasperated by the unwanted devotion and upon spotting me, she rolls her eyes upwards and tilts her head backwards at her brother.

I give her a sympathetic raise of my eyebrows and accompanying shoulder shrug. *What can you do?* I say to her in silence. Her faint smile back says she's reading me and there's *nothing* she can do.

The father looks utterly bored. He's lazing about, no doubt eye weary from roving through scores of t-shirt and novelty stores. The Sunsational chain alone (we call them T-Marts around here) is enough to break the disposition of even the most rabid souvenir hunter.

"Oooohhhh, Deadpool!" the boy shrieks, tearing away from his sister. She sends me a double fist pump, a temporary reprieve. We laugh to the air at each other.

"Isn't Owen a bit too young for that?" I hear the mother buzz to her husband, who's an easy ten paces away. She has competition between the music and a spouse who's found something to take his eyes away from her, and she *is* a bit of a stunner, as far as shell-shocked moms go. He's indifferent, already giving his unquestionably too young son a thumbs-up to the Deadpool shirt. I see the mother take the daughter with her out of the store as a means of protest. The father has a sudden change of mind and jerks his head at his Deadpool freak of a kid to give it up and move on.

On my inventory ledger next to the register, I mark off five shot glasses as damaged and disposed of. With the pen still in my hand, I find the point drifting to the flat desk calendar I have spread beneath the covered portion of the counter. I keep it there to keep track of Andrew and Rachel's work hours, as much for them as myself.

For whatever reason, I feel compelled to doodle. It's all so familiar, as I drag the pen into an upward perpendicular arc, making a curled tip before swooping back to the other side of the scrawling. To many, it might look like a shark fin. It's a rip curl, a wave. Damn, what brought that on? I haven't done one of those in years.

I feel embarrassed, so I scratch over it like I've already been caught until it's a full black smirch. I want nobody, Andrew and Rachel inclusive, to see what it was. Christ, no. I don't need them asking questions I don't want to answer. The mere thought sours my good mood, and there are no self-help mantras I can chant to undo the inexplicable funk hitting me suddenly. They talk about women's mood swings...

Another customer's wandered in, and he has that look about him, the one that says *Don't fucking bother me. I'll get you if I need help.* Sometimes those are the ones you must pay extra attention to before they slip some merchandise into the folds of their half-zippered jackets or extra baggy swim trunks. Most of them are what I call "No Sales," the tenacious, obtuse buyers who roam and weave for a spell before moving on without buying anything.

So I keep to myself and let him roam, leaving my leery eye to trail him.

Five minutes...six....seven...he's hanging out longer than your typical No Sale, which triggers my alarm bell. I'm wary of the guy, but I finish my last pretzel bite and I let myself think of Katya again while watching him. I already know that girl's on the first Megabus to New York as soon as she learns what one of those are. I'll make Katya autograph her cover spread on *Vanity Fair* for me one day and we'll laugh about Seafarer's and freebie soft pretzels.

"Hey there," I say to the roamer on minute eight. He's scanning the dangling decals from the ceiling, and I know he hasn't settled on any specific one. He's wearing olive cargo shorts and horrendous sandals I know he got at the boardwalk version of Five Below. He has on a cranberry polo shirt and a fishing-themed aquamarine Under Armour ball cap. He's as much a fisherman as I am, though I *could* be if I had the time.

It's so glaring he's single. What wife in good conscience (even Lady Firebug) would let her man on the loose in such a gaudy culture clash? He'd bought the cap a few blocks down at the surf shop, Coastal Breeze. I've tossed pints many times with the owner, Lenny Denforth. I know his stock as well as my own. Now I'm feeling cautious.

"Anything I can help you with?"

"I'm good, bud," he replies, not looking at me. "Just browsing."

A bit longer than your usual browser, I rationalize to myself, but I back off, adding *I'm surprised you're not wearing black crew socks to complete your train wreck ensemble.*

The store's gone silent as my Replacements playlist has reached the end of its queue. I swing away and go back to the store front, swiping on my laptop and dragging the music files toolbar until I settle on Social Distortion. I check on the guy in quick snap intervals.

So much so that I fail to spot another man slithering inside. It's so blatant, his slinky half-steps pegging him just as sketchy as Not-a-Fisherman. This one's far better dressed in khaki pants and a black Calvin Klein short sleeve that belches out his muscles. His fading hairline is marked by a severe buzz, and there's a stiffness to the way he moves which spikes the despondency hitting me moments ago.

He doesn't have the look of a shoplifter. For certain a No Sale if there ever was one, since I can tell he'd just as soon shop at a Sam's Club closedown than drop money in my place. He's casing the store, without a doubt, and not even Mike Ness' caterwauling about losing everything on a blackout summer night can keep me calm. It makes things worse. I'm grateful to myself for scratching away my blotter doodle.

Calvin Klein looks over at me and sends me a brief backwards tug of his head. From this bulging man, it's a provocation, not a salutation.

Now I want any excuse to close the store. I want to beg the manager to do it, but hell, that's me.

The two oddballs cross paths once, nod to each other and keep scanning around the store. It's clear as day neither one is interested in t-shirts or coffee mugs, nor the God-awful saltwater taffy. Candy Kitchen's is more expensive, but you can trust what they put into their taffy.

Andrew's due to come on shift at 4:00, a little more than an hour away. Rachel behind him at 5:00, my closer who is as reliable as what the Washington Nationals used to win a pennant before selling off the farm.

"What'cha think of this one?" Not-a-Fisherman asks. It's abrupt, and it startles me even more since he's not addressing me. He's holding a screen-printed, kid's sized tee with a cartoonish shark fin poking out of the waves, a water-bogged **OCEAN CITY** emblem dunked below the aquamarine sea surface.

Oh shit, I panic inside. I never thought this would happen, not after three decades in the perfect job to stay incognito. I can't believe it, but I've been made.

"Nah," Calvin Klein responds, and the way he drags out the rest of his sentence, I know I'm in huge trouble. "Not really Jacob's style."

"He's a four-year-old, sheesh," Not-a-Fisherman admonishes. "What does *he* care about style? He loves that annoying 'Baby Shark' song, is where I'm coming from."

"As his honorary uncle, I'm looking out for him," Calvin Klein gibes. "Look at the way his old man dresses. Who got you dressed anyway, Lew, that overly happy dude from *Blues Clues?*"

"Which one?" asks Not-a-Fisherman, now with a name of "Lew." Short for Lewis, I assume. "There's been a few of them."

Though they came in at different times, it's obvious they know each other. Fooled the hell out of me. These men aren't mere tourists. Their fraternal bashing of one another and the self-designation by Calvin Klein (whatever *his* real name is) as "honorary uncle" says they're connected. They're tight. It's got me quaking in my knees because the way Lew is dressed smells of undercover. Blown to hell undercover, but undercover, nonetheless.

"If you weren't a dad, I'd be worried about you, Lew. Of course, now I know why Sally left you."

"Oh, piss off," Lew scoffs, but there's no malice to his tone. Just a razz between guys who've been doing it a long time. There's such a comfort level to their banter it's like blind, comedic instinct.

"Heh," Calvin Klein guffaws before he looks my way. "Afternoon to you, sir."

I'm shaken like I'd just gotten the stuffing beat out of me on the Zipper ride down at the inlet. I'm off my game, out of my zone. I'm about to hurl before I can say single word.

The formality of his greeting to me, I don't like it. "Sir" is reserved for the more polite teenagers or people who've been brought up old school. Calvin Klein here, it's the way someone from the military or the police...a *detective* would say it. Official, straightforward, commanding –manipulating, even—of the situation.

I put up my hand as a half-hearted greeting. I try not to let them see the fear in my eyes, but I know I'm caught by the way Calvin Klein's eyes peer at me, like he's not really sizing me up, but confirming what he suspects about me.

He has a right to.

"You know what that shirt reminds me of, Lew?"

"What's that, Geoff?"

Finally, a name to the other guy. Lew and Geoff. These apparent investigators ought to have their own reality tv show. Lew and Geoff, Beach Detectives, I laugh to myself. It helps me put on a fake smile.

"You remember back in the day when we were in high school? Dave the Wave?"

Now I'm frozen. The only thing melting on me is the smile. All I want to do is drag the steel door down and run like hell. Closed until further notice. Good luck getting past the Harry W. Kelley Drawbridge on your way to New York City, Katya.

"Riiiiiiiight," Lew replies, fanning out the small shirt. "This is a shark fin, but yeah, I get where you're going. Those damn wave symbols were all over Maryland. Dave the Wave, ha! Wow, good flashback, man."

"You couldn't take a piss in any public men's room on Route 50 without looking at that damn wave graffiti."

"The summer after graduation," Lew says with a forced belly laugh making me even more uneasy. Makes me wonder if it's more of an interrogative precursor than shtick. "He got so into himself he started planting his mark *everywhere*. Grocery store bulletin boards, libraries, liquor stores, parks, public benches, underpasses..."

"I remember going to the nudie bars at The Block when we were underage, and they let us in anyway. They'd let *him* in too! That stupid wave was planted in one of the guy's room stalls!"

Not only detectives, but buddies from way back. The more I look at them, the more I realize we're in the same age bracket. My only question I keep to myself is, how they'd put it all together? Worse, was there anything they could do to me after all these years? Was there any statute of limitations to possible charges they could drum up?

"Exactly!" Lew interrupts. "Dave the Wave drew his trademark, real small-like, on the door handle to The Kat Club. We laughed the bouncer hadn't even noticed. Dave the Wave sightings became a sort of game back then. Dude had balls, I'll give him that."

"Last time anyone saw one of those wave drawings," Geoff says, so matter-of-factly I realize how far he's dug into this, "it was so long ago, but people spotted them in Philly, then the Jersey turnpike rest stops."

"Yep, that's what I heard too," Lew affirms, and now they're both looking at me. However I appear to them right now, I know they believe they have me cornered. Unless by some miracle Andrew's early for shift (a bigger long shot than an independent winning the next election, much less any), I'm screwed.

"Bird is the word," Geoff drones. "And Dave is the wave."

"I know I saw one of those wave avatars in a bathroom stall at the Philly Museum of Art," Lew adds. "Dude loved desecrating shitters for some reason."

"Isn't that how you met Sally?" Geoff mocks. "Got her number off the bathroom wall, like that Faster Pussycat song from about the same time Dave the Wave was prowling?"

"You can blow me, funny guy."

I wish I wasn't too petrified to enjoy their slapstick, but the guilty remembrance of placing my mark at the Philly Museum of Art long ago tells me I am royally screwed.

I have only one play and it isn't much.

"I'll give you a half-off discount on the shirt," I tell Lew. "You know, for your kid."

"Really?" Lew chirps, and I can tell he's pretending as much as I am. The power over the situation has shifted to his and Geoff's side. "I appreciate that, pal. Gonna have to pass, but thanks for the offer."

As Lew folds and replaces the shirt to its table display, Geoff resumes speaking, never once taking his eyes off of me.

"Everyone said Dave the Wave vanished to the eastern shore. Ocean City, no less."

Shit. Shit. *Shit.*

"If you believe the rumors," Lew says, taking the proverbial baton. Their act is flawless.

"I dunno, man," Geoff muses out loud. All a sport to these guys, and I'm losing in a hurry. "There are still 54 outstanding counts of vandalism against the guy after all these years. No wonder he bailed."

He pauses on purpose. He's dragging it out. He's sweating me.

Anyone who knows me in Ocean City knows me as Mark Metcalf. Really, though, it's...

"David Samonisky," Geoff states. It feels like incrimination as much as it sounds.

"Didn't we know a Dave Samonisky in school, Geoff?"

"Hmmmm," his partner responds. I see both of his biceps twitch and his eyes widen. It's like Geoff's preparing for a cage brawl. He's trying to rile me. I don't recall going to school with either of these guys, but it's been so long. If they make the direct accusation, it's going to take everything I have not to admit I'm Dave the...

"Never mind," Lew pretend-gruffs. He's enjoying himself so much I nearly blurt it out. "I'm thinking of Dave *Smalls*."

"Right, Dave Smalls," Geoff verifies with a rugged, lip-pursing nod.

Inside, I exhale, but I feel nowhere near safe.

"Yeah, the guy went off the grid, good for him," Lew says, now in smug tone. "Nobody knows what happened to him. Prince George's County smokeys state they have two guys of note named David Samonisky. One is assumed to be Dave the Wave. The other got a job as a talent scout for the Cleveland Browns. Cleared his background check and all. Guy's finally doing his job after all those losing seasons, heh."

"You ever hear of Dave the Wave, pal?" Lew asks me and I think of hilarious scenes in comedy films where big, bruising hulks of men scream like little girls. It's what I want to do right now. "If there's one town that guy decorated like it was his personal turf, it was here in Ocean City. Kinda fits the vibe, at least."

The question shakes me up again and all I can do is pretend like I'm searching my memory banks. The pretzel bites Katya brought me feels like a pile of rocks in my gut, the cheesy dip like burning lava. I know it's not going to take much longer before I need to bolt for the bathroom because I'm churning.

"Sure, I've seen those wave doodles before," I muster. Doodles. That's my word. I can't ever call them anything else. It was a habit, an addiction, dumb stuff you do when you're young and indomitable. Yeah, I went hog wild when I'd moved here, but the more settled I got at Ocean City, the more it felt like home. So much I legally changed my name. I thought it had been overkill then, the way a paranoiac would act, but now I see how right I'd been to trust my instincts.

Only then did my "wave" doodles feel like actual defacing. Like you would be having to get off drugs, I forced myself to stop drawing them. Nowhere near as drastic as classic substance withdrawal symptoms, I learned to push my fixation into the heat presses whenever I'd iron a decal. It's why I take pleasure doing it so much.

Thinking about the wave doodle I did before the detectives came in, it was like what my English Language Arts and Literature teachers called foreshadowing. A subconscious part of me knew this was coming sometime. It had taken decades for someone to put the pieces together. I'd thought the whole thing had blown over. Why it mattered to these investigators like Dave the Wave was some unsolved cold case, that disturbed me the most.

"Been a while, though, right?" Lew asks, still baiting me.

"Yeah," I answer, still trying to remain cool. "Long time since I last saw those."

"Yeah, long time," Geoff concurs and I'm even more agitated than when I put the detectives' roles together.

Do either of them have handcuffs? Are they going to drag me out of the store like a fugitive? God help me, don't let Katya see any of this. Crazy to think, who's going to keep watch over the store before Andrew comes on shift?

"Last I heard about Dave Smalls," Lew interposes in such a nonchalant manner I realize it's all being played to a script. "The guy flipped out being accused of the Dave the Wave marks he started doing them himself, but that was years later."

"A copycat scribbler, isn't that the damnedest thing?" Geoff quipped, looking at me like he was waiting for me to corroborate before asking for real. "Don't you think so, pal?"

I let my nervous smile serve as the only answer I had.

"Once Smalls got caught doing it at a funeral home in Bowie, of all places," Lew went on, "he paid for the damages, those he would fess up to. PG County was satisfied they'd put a face to Dave the Wave and held him accountable to thirteen counts of public nuisance and vandalism charges."

"Any face being sufficient," Geoff notes.

"Dave the Wave, for all intents and purposes, settled his debt and went away. Well, as far as Crofton. It may or may not have been the original guy, who knows? Nobody gives a rat's ass since most of the victims were able to clear his marks away."

That was my logic back then. Yeah, I used black permanent marker, but it came off with a little extra scrubbing. I should know. I did it to myself years after I stopped, just to be sure.

"We done here, Lew?" Geoff asks his partner, now swerving around the store as if he'd really come in to shop. "We're off-duty, I'm thirsty, and you're buying at Big Kahuna's."

"You're only partially right," Lew says back. "We're going to Seafarers and it's *your* treat."

"Take care of yourself, ahh," Geoff prompts me with his outstretched hand.

"Metcalf," I tell him, meeting his hand with mine and hoping I apply enough force to pass off my dwindling trepidation. "Mark Metcalf."

"*Right,*" Lew says in a droll tone letting me know he sees through my bluff. It's Geoff who pulls the proverbial curtain down on my charade.

"You run a store called Wave Runner Tees & Souvenirs, Mr. Metcalf? Seriously? Brother, you've got all the gods on your side if we're the only ones who figured it out. *Wave Runner?* Bigger calling card than you used to leave. Checkmate, my friend."

My mouth hangs open and I can't think of a thing to say. I'm waiting for the Miranda warning, but it doesn't come.

"Take it easy, pal," Lew tells me. "If we were going to bust you, the shields would be out already. Call this satisfaction of a long-running curiosity."

"We just had to know," Geoff adds. I can feel the definitive period stamp his statement. Mike Ness drones overhead how much he wants someone to take away the ball and chain and only then do I exhale.

"What he said," Lew adds.

"Next time you wear an Under Armour hat," Geoff teases his partner as they drift out of the store, "get one without fishhooks. Just saying."

If the gods have indeed favored me, they're not giving me much time to absorb what's just happened as I'm tackled in place.

"Mark! Mark!"

If she had the strength to match her height, Katya could pick me up, yet she squeezes me and kisses me twice on both cheeks, then unlatches herself. Now she's bouncing up and down using her hands on my shoulders for leverage. Like a daughter getting a college acceptance letter, only better.

"I got invite!" she squeals.

"To what?" I ask, trying to brush off the staggering events of the past twenty minutes. It's a gear shift change I don't think I'm capable of until I look at the beam on Katya's face. Then I understand.

"My portfolio! Model agency! Mark, they want to meet me! *New York!*"

"Here you come," I tell Katya with as much pride as I can shove out.

Her hug comes with zealous dancing in place while trapping herself in my arms. She counters the sluggish drag of Social D, making "Ball and Chain" seem like a popping EDM number in her world. Once she breaks free, I can't resist myself.

With my forefinger, I draw a wave symbol in the air.

"GLAD WE RAN THAT 10K *before* coming here," Kate said, coughing a few times while taking half breaths and squinting through the grayish murk of the townhouse. "I'll never complain again about that musty cave off the Clarion River we tramped through in my Earth Science class."

"I warned you."

"You weren't kidding, Scott, *wow* it's hard to breathe in here," Kate added, pulling off her pink Adidas ball cap and pulling her sandy curls loose of a matching-colored hair tie. Her tresses bounced free and cascaded down her neck, which was carrying a film of sweat. Without any air conditioning running in the townhouse, the air was sweltering as much as it was smoggy.

"No poor reflection on you, but how could anyone live in these conditions? It's obvious he was not one to open a window. Please tell me he didn't have any pets."

"Luckily, no," Scott replied, scrunching his face from the smoky stench punching into his nostrils and down his throat. Like his girlfriend of only three months, he rasped through the omnipresent tobacco clog. "I never lived here, thank God. My mother divorced him when I was only eight. Had he raised me, I doubt you would've said yes when I asked you out."

"You loved him, anyway."

"Of course, I did," Scott affirmed, reaching for the foyer light switch and flicking it on. The clicking noise echoed within the soundless gloom. "He did a ripe number on me as a kid and up to his death; the chain-smoking old goat could still put me through the wringer when he wanted to. Dying alone and like the way he did...it takes away any appeal of solitary living."

"It was his choice," Kate said, placing a soothing hand upon Scott's shoulder and giving him a one-time squeeze before tickling the fade of the close-buzzed hairline on his neck. "You said it yourself more than once in the little time I've known you."

"True."

The swish of Kate's bundled curls as she ran could melt him inside of his running shorts, as could her assortment of black, maroon, and royal blue leggings with the purposeful hosed-covered slits exposing the calves. Today for the Nita Bandera Foundation 10K race, Kate had chosen slate gray leggings. At least until she'd pulled away from Scott after the second mile, he'd held onto a magnificent view of her firm buttocks showcased in that pair. Only by a peppering of life's seasoning to her hardy, sage face could you tell Kate had crossed the gates of midlife. Forty-eight years old with only a few telltale wrinkles, but clocking a terrific 1:03:32 in the race, she was giving the proverbial gatekeeper a vigorous flip-off on her way through.

Kate's athletic leggings were further adorned with hip pockets to carry her iPhone13, which she used to monitor her running progress using her trusted mile and step counter apps. It was tucked in there right now. Ever since coming to Scott's father's place, Kate's phone had dinged five times with text message indicators and social media notifications. Truth be told, her customized soundbyte pings from the *Chocolat* film score had started to grind on Scott's nerves after three months of dating. A point in Kate's favor, she'd affixed a separate ringtone for his incoming calls, set to a romantic spool of electronic chimes from Hans Zimmer and Benjamin Wallfisch's lush, synthesized *Blade Runner 2049* soundtrack, "Rain."

Kate was the fastest texter he'd ever seen in any age bracket, much less her being three years his junior. Even though she could be glued to the damn thing (answering incoming messages when they were about to make love on two occasions), Kate's iPhone hyperactivity was countered by a sweeping personality filled with charm, wit, and a warrior spirit, all of which turned him on.

"I thought we were going to need a shower from running," Kate uttered. "It might take a full hour to scrub this filth away. Your old man, not much of a housekeeper."

"He thought Brillo was what you laid your head on to go to sleep," Scott cracked. He took short breaths, more than half of what he'd gulped in intervals during the race.

"I'll pretend I didn't hear that."

Despite the tobacco reek pummeling her lungs, Kate glanced at Scott and gave him her pluckiest grin. Sensing her discomfort, Scott wrapped his arm around Kate and pulled her close to drop a peck on her cheek.

"All these years, you'd think I'd be used to it, but I still get all mucked up being in here."

"Muck's a good word," Kate returned, waving her hand back and forth in front of her face.

His father had first moved into the place back in 1991. What used to be a solid white paint to the walls inside the townhouse had eroded to a vomit palette, congested by an endless barrage of secondhand cigarette smoke. It was a trend carrying throughout the entire townhouse. Even with the gritty facade of the slate terrazzo in the foyer, it was evident no mop had touched the tiles in years. Scott shook his head with an outward sigh.

Ancient cobwebs cast by long-dead spiders of the past dangled from the ceiling. Pointing up to the garish strands, Scott said, "If that's not repulsive enough for you, check out the bug cemeteries he left on the windowsills."

"Rank," Kate groaned.

"See that?" Scott asked her, indicating a once tropical-colored fuzzy duster left for dead on the floor near the half bath just feet away from the main door. "I gave him that for the webs."

"When, at the turn of millennium?" Kate joked with a short laugh gulped by a cough.

"Sounds about right," Scott said in a serious manner.

"You're kidding me."

"The old man never did make use of the gifts I gave him, many of them things he himself had asked for. The duster, for one. I mean, why, if you're not going to use it? In the kitchen is a Fry Daddy I gave him more than twenty years ago, still in its box. He'd spent nearly an hour telling me how a George Foreman half grill would make cooking easier for him. Funny, when you consider he only ate the same six or seven meals and none of them were steaks or hamburgers. Last I checked, you put a meat loaf into an oven, not on a grill. That being one of his six or seven meals."

"Sheesh," Kate said with a roll of her eyes. Scott could see they were starting to burn.

"The man was eccentric. I don't apologize for him."

"Nor should you, babe."

"In his bedroom closet are a bunch of short-sleeve dress shirts. Lavender, peach and sky blue. Those colors only, all on hangers, all of which still have their cardboard collar supporters in them. He never used any of them, though it's how he dressed, even at home, like he was always at work. It'd be hilarious if it wasn't so damned weird."

"I'm not sure he didn't have a touch of Nikola Tesla in him, Scott. Don't ask me where I just got *that* from, other than my professor from the same science class during sophomore year at Happy Valley."

"Were you a Lady Lion track star back in the day?"

"Actually, my passion for running came after I'd graduated. I spent a lot of my college time in the company of my sorority sisters from Alpha Phi Delta. We were always knee-deep in some fundraising or local charity project when we weren't blitzed out of our minds at the Skeller."

"What's that, a bar?"

"The All-American Rathskeller, a Penn State institution of higher drinking."

"Cheers; we had a Rathskeller too in the common area at Salisbury University. 'The Rat,' we called it. No alcohol, but good for a pizza when you needed one during cram sessions."

"Well, *boo.* I think they closed the original location at Pugh Street and might've re-opened somewhere else. I'll take you with me on an expedition sometime. Get a few drinks in me for old times' sake, I just might share some stories to roll your socks. Of course, since you wear *ankle* socks, the stories might be abbreviated."

Scott's immediate laughter was intercepted by a ripping cough sounding as painful as it had felt.

"You alright?" Kate asked him, clapping his back but not too hard.

"Not by a mile. Now check out this vinyl tablecloth, still in its packaging and never put into play to replace the grody Colonial pattern tablecloth you can see on his kitchen table right now. The old one's all shredded and burned to shit from his cigarettes. I'm positive it's the same one he'd taken with him when he and my mom split up. I recall eating bowls of Franken Berry cereal as a kid with that pattern beneath me. It had color then."

"Whaaaaaat?" Kate quipped. "When would you last say he actually *cleaned* in here?"

"Funny you should ask. Try a quarter of a century ago when Carly and I pounded through here, top-to-bottom. We were only engaged then. Dad stroked us three hundred to do it. We put a deposit down on the wedding cake with that."

"I hope you shoved it in her face at the reception."

"No, but she did it to me."

"Grounds for immediate annulment if you ask me. Who came up with that dumb tradition, anyway?"

"It's above and beyond you came, Kate," Scott told her, swerving away from their current sidebar. He wanted to twirl his forefinger into one of her curls. Seeing his intention, she dipped her head to let him.

"I couldn't imagine you coming in here alone, so soon after finding him the way you did."

"I'll never un-see that for the rest of my years."

Kate raised her head from Scott, then glided her palm down his spine and back up, tracing each of his cut shoulder blades.

"You know, I'd bet my entire inheritance—what's left of it—the man never once sat on that couch and chair. Look at it, still immaculate and smooth, though the dyes have taken a beating from the smoke. No indentations, creases or any hint they'd been used. He'd been so proud when he'd bought those pieces."

"They'd be at home in a county taxation office, maybe. Yick."

"In the basement, you'll find my high school senior portrait upside down in a box of scraps I figure he'd intended to throw out but never did. I'd paid for the whole set of pictures on my own. I was 17, on a grocery clerk's pittance. Once you take away the gas and car insurance money, even by 1980s standards, there wasn't a ton left."

"Aww, Scott, how could he be so mean?"

Wrapping her arms around him from behind, Kate held onto Scott, laying her cheek against his shoulder.

"Maybe because I had long hair in that picture, which he never liked. Called me a fag more than once whenever he tied one on."

"Jesus, what a bastard."

"We're not gonna stay much longer," Scott told her, grabbing her hands and pulling them across his chest. "If it's killing me to be in here, I can't imagine what it does to someone who's not used to it."

"I'll deal, Scott, just let me be here for you."

"Thanks. No need for a full tour since one look into his toilets and bathtubs will scar you for life. Let me get the most important thing I need, which is this box with all his post-death instructions. He always kept it in the kitchen."

"Whatever you need."

"I need to get the hell out of here," Scott said with a growl, letting Kate's arms go limp. "After that, I need a shower, more than one drink, and maybe we can grab some Caribbean for an early dinner?"

"As long that's a shower for two, I'm down for all of it."

"You're my kind of a lady."

Scott stepped through the single open walkway between the living room and adjacent dining room, which hooked into the kitchen. Already knowing where it was, he reached out to his right without looking in its direction and flipped on another light switch, filling the dining room with a garish brightness.

"Good God," Kate grunted as she could see a hoard of boxes and flotsam in front of her. "Your dad seriously could've used a *Buried Alive* intervention."

The dining room was log-jammed with hip-high piles of beat-up cartons and trash bags stuffed with papers. In the middle was an oak dining room set, the table overloaded with more boxes, old newspapers, unopened mail, and draped across the back of a table chair, an old North Carolina Tar Heels coat from the time Michael Jordan played there.

"He used to collect baseball cards," Scott said, pointing to a tier of cased baseball card sets from the years 1992 through 1995. "Thought he could get some serious coin for them."

"There's being a pack rat and there's...*this*."

"There's still time to bail, Kate. After today, I won't take offense."

"Against my better judgment, I'll give it another month and see what happens."

"Nice," Scott retorted with a warm laugh this time as he veered into the kitchen. "You want might want to hang back. The kitchen is beyond gross, and this is where we spent most of the time when I'd visit, eating the same reheated spaghetti leftovers he'd serve and hearing the same old war stories of his career at Social Security."

"I think I'll take you up on it. I can't even imagine what you two would eat off."

"He washed his dishes, I'll give him that. Although he'd put them to dry in his dishwasher and left it open 24-7, just like it is right now. He only used the same handful of plates, utensils, and cups."

"Is calling him a nut job out of line?"

"I'll only be a minute. Dad's wishes were to be cremated and he asked me all the way back in my early twenties to scatter his ashes at Deep Creek. He gave me a vague idea where, but I'll need a map to find it."

"Your dad's a pain in the ass and I've never even met him," Kate said to Scott's back.

Knowing where to go, even with faint illumination from the dining room, Scott paused a moment and sighed as he surveyed from the shadows two piles of *Turf* horse racing magazines nearly as tall as he was. They dated back to the early 1990s. His eyes watered in sadness to see that off-color, gold ashtray, loaded with crushed cigarette butts. Next to it was two cartons of Salems, one sealed and one unfinished pack stacked on top of each other. A yellow Bic lighter sat linear to them.

"You could be tidy when you wanted to," Scott mumbled. "You supreme asshole."

"What'd you say, Scott?" Kate called from the dining room.

"Nothing important. Fucking Salems. Fucking COPD. Fucking waste of a life."

"Salem? I don't mean to be rude and I've never smoked anything but a spliff now and then, but isn't that considered a girl's brand of cigarette?"

"He also drank a girlie beer, Schlitz."

"I'll pretend I didn't hear that either."

Beneath the kitchen table, near a pair of battered moccasin-styled slippers and with a huge cake of grit leading up to them, there was the mud-colored box in question.

The banker's box was at least forty years old, by Scott's recollection. He remembered it being around as a kid, well before his parents divorced, first brought home by his mother during her time as a teller at the long-folded First National Bank of Hampton. The box was sturdy given its age and the weight of the contents inside. With a sticky sounding resistance from being in the same spot for ages, the box came with a firm tug.

Scott inhaled and at once choked. His hands shook. In the past five years, his father had often reminded him the box was there in the event of his death. There was always mention of it, followed by the preamble that all its contents would outline Scott's duties as his father's intended personal representative of the estate. Considering his dad had no known relatives on speaking terms with him nor any friends outside of a bar, Scott considered himself de facto.

Scott glanced away for just a moment at a spot near the open dishwasher where he'd found his dad, sprawled on the floor. A pool of dried blood had spread around his father's bashed and sunken-in head. Trying to put the events together inside his head, Scott's father had either tripped or blacked out and struck his head on the way down. Against the countertop, against the gaped open dishwasher door, Scott couldn't tell. No traceable dents or blood in those spots.

After his father's body had been removed and the police had asked a bunch of questions Scott had no answers for, he'd mopped the blood once no foul play had been determined. Scott could only imagine the revulsion of the forensics team, not from the blood, but the filth in which they had to work. He then thought for just a moment with dread at what might show on his father's death certificate as a possible immediate and underlying cause once that was finished. The underlying irony to Scott right now was the scrubbed spot was the only spic and span spot to be found anywhere in the house.

"You okay in there, Scott?"

"Sure," he lied, feeling sick to his stomach.

A gritty stretch of masking tape had been placed upon the lid. Looking like it had been written long ago in a fading black marker, he saw his name: "SCOTT."

As he pulled the lid free, he saw stacks of papers, some on loose-leaf with his father's jagged style of cursive only Scott, to his knowledge, could decipher. There were loads of firmer parchment, all with the embossed header of **The Law Offices of Lucius Jackson, P.A.** These, Scott, presumed, were related to his father's will and administrative documentation. A tug with his forefinger of the first few pages and there it was, live ink and notary seal. The will. Scott took only a second to glance at it to make sure his name was on it. Like he needed to.

Already Scott was growing dizzy from the burden thrust upon him. How was he going to get this shithole of a townhouse cleaned, fumigated and repainted so he could drop it on the market? Was there enough left in his father's accounts for such a cumbersome project, or would Scott have to take a loss and sell it outright to a rehab investor?

Scott wanted to leave the goddamn box where it was, take Kate by the hand, and dart right the hell out of there. If it wasn't a townhouse where the connected occupants would suffer, he'd be tempted to take that stinking cigarette lighter and light the whole place up.

He was about to close the box when he spotted something out of place with the rest of the contents.

It was a spiral notebook, one a student would use in school. It had a blaring red cover, remarkably effervescent amidst the ashy pallor of its surroundings.

Though he was scrambling in his mind for any excuse to leave, Scott couldn't avoid it. What was this notebook?

His hands still trembling, Scott opened the notebook and unlike the box lid and the will, was he startled this time to see his name as the first word. What he read from there planted him knees-down to the floor:

Scott, I know I could've been a better father to you. Your mother and Larry did a wonderful job raising you. For years, I was jealous I couldn't be a part of your daily life, but I know now I wasn't suited for parenthood. Things happened the way they were supposed to. Always know that I love you, even with what I have to tell you.

If you're reading this, it means I'm dead and I apologize for doing this in such a cowardly way. I tried so hard to dig deep and say this to your face. Every time that urge came, I would run to this notebook and write a little bit more each time, until I left you my full confession.

Son, what you'll read next will shake you up and I apologize in advance. I know you'll have enough on you when I die but know I regret it all and wish I'd had a chance to atone for it. It just wasn't possible, but if I leave my admission behind, I'm hoping my conscience will at least have been served right in the afterlife, if nothing else.

Please don't judge me too harshly.

"Try and relax."

"I thought I *was* relaxed."

"Scott, I've seen third graders amped on ice cream more relaxed than you."

Scott chuckled from the folds of the pillow swallowing his face. Kate was mounted atop him at the waist as she worked her fingers and thumbs into each of his bare shoulder blades.

"Man, you're strong," he grunted, arching his neck just enough to breathe in and out. He winced a couple times once she'd found a knot with her thumb. She concentrated with the full purpose of unraveling it.

"It's like you had deltoid and triceps day all week long, you poor thing."

"That was last Wednesday, when I found Dad after my workout..."

"Shh, let it go for now."

Scott was gaining even more appreciation for Kate's forceful grip which not only rubbed; she hunted down the tension clusters burrowed beneath his skin. The lilac oil she'd brought in her overnight bag filled Scott's nostrils. The oil tingled against his skin, already sinking into the deeper tissues the harder Kate worked it in there. He could feel lumps he'd had no idea were there, resisting her fingers, then popping and yielding to her.

"Scott Secret for you," he groaned like he'd sunken full into the mattress with no intent of getting back up.

"Ahh, I suppose you'll be wanting a Kate Confidential in exchange?"

"Your prerogative. That oil of yours reminds me of the days when I was fond of unscrewing the lids to candle jars and sniffing them. Carly used to entrap me in craft shops or Bath and Body Works all the time. I needed something to do."

"Carly *who?*" Kate scoffed.

"I dunno, some ghost from my past," he answered with a pleased rumble as Kate worked out another kink at the top of his spine.

"Let's keep that ghost where it belongs. You know, Scott, for an old man, you sure are a rock."

"You give a hell of a massage, but really, *old man?* You have the hands of life, but your mouth is your superpower, Kate."

The fleshy crack of Kate's hand across his right rear cheek ricocheted around Scott's bedroom. She'd been quick swinging up her right hand and unloading the spank upon him, while keeping her left hand digging into the base of his neck.

Scott was fully naked upon his bed while Kate was still clothed in baggy blue flannel bottoms and a matching tank top, both bearing the snarling Nittany Lion avatar for Penn State University.

They'd left the bedroom television on mute. From the top of a cedar chest of drawers was a 19-inch flat screen where lawyers comically battled in silence through an old episode of *Law and Order.* The remote sat in front of the tv between two emptied Ramona artisanal wine coolers, crushed by both consumers in mere minutes. Scott tried not to let his burps leak from his lips as Kate ground her hands into him, though he was getting annoyed having to lock tangs of grapefruit secretions behind his lips.

"It's been a long time since I've given a man a rubdown."

"Been a long time since I've *gotten* one," Scott returned, once he was sure he wouldn't belch first. "Not one of Carly's specialties. Whenever I used to ask for one, she'd act like I was asking her to build a shed in the back yard all by herself. I'd get the bare minimum. You'll forgive me if I milk this as long I can."

"Not that I don't want to hear about everything in your life," Kate said, resuming her kneading with both hands," but I've had a bad track record of attracting emotional tampons who've gouged my ears about how awful their past women were. Fair warning, my patience meter for ex talk is slim."

"Warning taken," Scott said, letting a soft whirr emit from his lips.

"Did you just purr at me?" Kate giggled.

"Maybe. I'm not complaining, mind you, but it's Sunday. I know it's a work night for you. You don't have to be here."

"Just like I didn't have to come to your dad's place, but so what? It's my choice. I'm where I want to be. We have a light schedule in the morning, only one meeting to go over the launch campaign for the Connell Hardware account. My afternoon is stacked heavy, but why worry about *then* when *now* is a lot more appealing with a bare-assed man sprawled between my legs? Now shut up and enjoy."

"Sassy, I like it," Scott retorted with a laugh.

"Of course, you do. I had you pegged right off the bat. Do you have any assignments this week? I mean, you just lost your dad, Scott. Why don't you ask for some time off? I'm sure your editor will understand."

"Maybe," Scott said, feeling a slaver of drool leak from his mouth. He licked it gone with a flicker of his tongue before Kate could spot it. "I've already put Sam on alert I'm going to be busy this coming week with Dad's affairs."

"Will Sam do you a solid with the obit?"

"Definitely. Now that the funeral plans are made, Sam's already offered and I'm taking him up on it. Enjoy the irony, Dad. Perks of the writing life. You can't get *that* from the ledger trenches."

"He wasn't much of a supporter of your writing, I take it?"

"He wanted me to be an accountant, yuck."

"The stench on that banker's box," Kate diverted, easing her hands to a series of glides. She lifted her left and shook then rolled it a few times, working out a sudden kink of her own. "*Yuck.* Glad you left it on the porch."

Because of the years bombarded by cigarettes, once extracted into an outdoor element, the banker's box gave off a reek equivalent to a dead animal. Both Scott and Kate had become nauseated by the smoky smell the box dealt upon pulling it out of the trunk of Scott's beige Subaru. It was mutually decided to air the box outside for the night before attending to the unpleasant business within it. Scott had even left the trunk open a few hours by the mere suspicion of leftover congestion, even if it had only been a twenty minute drive from his dad's place to his own.

Not that he was ready to talk about it to Kate yet, Scott was still shaken up by that notebook. In particular, the confession his father had left behind.

What had his father *done?*

"It won't be much of a funeral," Scott said instead, trying to forget the box and the notebook for the time being. "Unless Dad's old work comrades and barfly buddies read the obituary, I doubt anyone will come."

"I'll be there."

"Don't lose time at work, Kate. I've got this. You didn't know the guy, and I don't expect you to ask for time…"

"Like hell," she interjected with a fierceness to her smile Scott already knew was there without seeing her. "And don't tell me what to do."

"You care for me this much already," Scott stated more than asked as he flipped himself over once Kate scooched off him and onto the side of his bed.

"Yes, I do, and that's my Kate Confidential for the day."

"There's something I didn't tell you when we were at the townhouse earlier."

"What's that?" Kate quipped, furrowing her eyebrows.

"Everything I thought I knew about that guy..."

"What?"

"He lived alone for so long and it's not like I was privy to his daily business."

"Scott...*what?*"

"Why should I even be surprised? That infuriating son of a bitch."

"Jesus, Scott, what is it?"

"I'll tell you in the morning, okay? I'll even make you the best omelet you've ever had since I know you love them. It's one of Larry's recipes. Onions and red peppers with dashes of cumin and chili powder. The Early Bird Kicker, he calls it. Right now, I'm enjoying the moment and I'm glad you want to stay the night. I know I'm jerking you around, but would you be mad if I asked to table this mess until tomorrow?"

"Alright," Kate said with a half-smirk saying she wasn't wholly pleased by Scott's diversion, but she would let things lie for the moment. "I spied a slab of turkey bacon thawing in your fridge. Hint

hint."

"Thawing with you in mind," Scott said, squeezing both of Kate's hands which grasped his.

For someone so light, Kate was so *solid*. She used her leverage from the bedside and pushed Scott back against the mattress, climbing up once again until she was in a kneeling position. This time her strategic straddle found his eager response where their groins met.

Scott stared into Kate's olive-green eyes, eyes showing as much calm and assurance as he could. He knew how he really looked.

"Aww," Kate said, grabbing the hem of her tank top. "That just might be the most pathetic face I've ever seen."

Scott guffawed, then let his smile become more concrete as the tank top lifted overtop Kate's head, her curls jiggling with her petite breasts, both of which rippled once, then settled. He lifted his left hand to cup her.

"I have another Kate Confidential for you," she told him, pressing his hand against her chest and then leaning down to whisper into his ear.

"Well, now," Scott said with a dirty grin.

The following morning, Kate's perfume was lofting inside Scott's bathroom an hour after she'd left for work. She'd tried a new scent, accenting her neck and cleavage with the vanilla-sandalwood-violet fragrance of "Nirvana Black" by Elizabeth & James. By contrast, Carly, who had as much scent sensibility as she did her fuddy-duddy choice in dress scarves, had sickened Scott more than once dousing herself in Clinique Aromatics Elixir. There was a reason the mothball-tanged crap was often called "Old Lady in a Bottle."

Before his meeting with Lucius Jackson, his father's estate planner, Scott found himself swabbing strands of Kate's coiled hair from his tub drain. Instead of pissing and moaning under his breath about it as he had for years with Carly's castaway follicle wads, Scott enjoyed having a reason to mop out hair again.

His cell phone pinged with a text from Kate.

Glad I left early. Turns out I have to put out a fire this morning. Two typos in a press release for my client, Addison Orthopedics. Our newbie copywriter failed to catch them, so I get to clean his mess, yipee. I don't know if it falls under the nepotism umbrella, but maybe I should put your name in the hat for a now-vacant freelancing spot.

Scott sent Kate a smiley emoji wearing a pair of cool guy shades, then, letting himself get caught away, he added the message:

Miss me already?

He didn't need wait long a response.

I can neither confirm nor deny, sir.

It was as fun and subtly sneaky as passing handwritten love notes to a school crush in class. Faster than usual for him, Scott pounded and sent his reaction to Kate.

Scott Secret, I keep smelling your perfume and I want a repeat performance of last night.

A few seconds later, she'd responded:

Kate Confidential, all part of the plan.

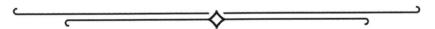

At 9:08 a.m. Scott found himself losing his hand to the sizable paw of

Lucius Jackson, Esquire. A bear of a man who'd no doubt been twice as formidable before he'd turned the page into his seventh decade of life, Lucius still wore the frame (albeit an older, soggier version) of a linebacker who'd made it through two years on the college level before tearing his tibial tendon and ending any hopes of a professional football life.

Instead, Lucius had made legal work his second calling and he'd risen to prominence as one of the first black lawyers in Baltimore to earn a six-figure salary back in the mid-1970s. A self-made man with as tight a grip over his personal finances, Lucius had never succumbed to the swank and the glitz of building a power firm. For the entire 43 years of his practice, the staff roster comprising The Law Office of Lucius Jackson, P.A. never surpassed seven. Following himself, Lucius employed one partner lawyer, his cousin, Carlton. He kept on the payroll three paralegals, a filing clerk and his receptionist, Tobie, who had been with him the longest of anyone, all but four of the firm's years of existence. These things, Tobie had conveyed to Scott while he waited for Lucius' arrival to the office.

In the lobby was a framed picture of younger, slimmer versions of Lucius and Tobie, back in the resistance age of the 1960s, both pumping upraised Panther fist salutes. What stood out the most to Scott was the cut definition to both of their forearms, as fiery as their enraged expressions. Next to that was a framed Stax Records 45 platter for Rufus Thomas' "The Breakdown," the finger snapping label autographed in gold marker by The Funkiest Man himself.

It was a wonder to Scott that at age 75, long past retirement age, Lucius was refusing to give up the reins. The heaps of manila file folders on each side of his cherry wood desk were intimidating even for a junior legal eagle clocking all the billable hours necessary to campaign for partnership.

"Good to meet you, finally, Scott," Lucius said in a husky-raspy, sophisticated voice. Like Billy Dee Williams might sound wrestling through strep throat. "Sad it's under these circumstances."

"You too, sir," Scott said, releasing his hand from Lucius's and trying not to marvel at the diamond-punched gold rings around four of the man's meaty fingers.

"As my own father who fought in the Korean conflict used to tell me, don't call me 'sir.' I work for a living."

"Good enough, Mr. Jackson."

"Come on, now, it's Lucius. I'm sorry for your loss, Scott. Your father was a good man."

"Thank you, Lucius," Scott said, letting his thoughts drift for a moment. *That's speculative. You only saw one side of the guy, my guess.*

"I first met your father ages ago at Wake Park. I was playing golf with two friends of mine, but they refused to send us out unless we were a foursome. The tee starter there wasn't your most enlightened fella in the world. Many pairs went out before us, all *white*, of course. We didn't take too much offense until a trio of white men were allowed out by that surly tee starter. Your father came to the course alone and he had no qualms whatsoever joining up with three men of color. We hit it off, since it turned out your father worked in Social Security's version of the EEOC."

"Right," Scott said with a nod, taking a seat in front of Lucius and planting the stack of files he'd brought along for the meeting into his lap. It all still reeked of secondhand smoke. The notebook, he'd left behind.

"Anyway, as unpleasant as this may be for you to hear, your father was looking to divorce your mother..."

It was the other way around, Scott growled to himself.

"He retained me, and I represented him back then. Obviously, he's been a repeat client since you and I are here today to discuss his estate matters."

"Yeah," Scott acknowledged, trying to plant a congenial smile on his face and struggling with it.

"Right, then," Lucius said, grabbing the top file from his left side. "So, your dad passed testate, meaning he left a will naming you as his intended personal representative of his property and assets."

You should actually see *his property and assets,* Scott thought, feeling his eyebrows raise as he traipsed a mental inventory of his father's ramshackle home.

"I'm not sure how familiar you are with probate law..."

"Only a little," Scott answered, opening his father's file and pulling a copy of the same will Lucius was looking at.

"He left you an original, good. That'll help cut through the explanation, assuming you've read it all."

"Bathroom reading material," Scott joked with a lame smirk. Lucius didn't appear to be amused.

"The first step is to determine the value of your father's worth, and that would be classified as either a small or regular estate. The court will go by the fair market value of all your dad's property, less all known debts he might've incurred. Do you have a general idea of what debts he might've had?"

"Not really, other than his mortgage. He didn't use plastic and I know he sneered at credit lines. I'm not sure what, if any, balance is left on his car, which is a 2015 Scion. I really don't know, Lucius. He was a private man, as I'm sure you know."

"Yes," Lucius confirmed, rifling through his copies of the paperwork. "Then your dad should have a regular estate, which is fairly simple. I know it'll be a tough process going through his belongings and placing a monetary value to it, but once you've come up with that figure, we'll run credit and background checks. Make sure you check thoroughly for any outstanding debts."

"Got it."

"In the meantime, we'll petition the court to name you as his Personal Representative and we'll post the bond. The Notice of Appointment will go out, and any creditors we haven't found have six months to file their claims. That's all the first part of the process and I'll guide you along as time progresses. Gather what you think may be of material value and send me an inventory."

"He didn't really keep a lot of stuff I'd consider valuable," Scott said. "If anything, it'd be considered *de*valued. You don't want to see his place firsthand, trust me."

He didn't expect himself to open up any further, but the soft expression upon so large of a man as Lucius made Scott feel more comfortable than he expected.

"Snap pictures of anything that looks solvent. I know it's a tedious task, but if you can list all the items as best you can, I'll need it."

"It's just going to be a heck of a job. You don't know how the man lived the past twenty-some years. The clean-up alone will eat up a lot of his reserves, I'm afraid, much less keeping up the mortgage until it can be paid off through resale."

"I understand," Lucius said, standing up with a noticeable effort. "I have some papers for you to sign before you leave."

For a moment, the red notebook sprang to Scott's mind. Did Lucius know anything about what it might entail? Scott felt the urge to ask sizzling the edge of his tongue. If his father and Lucius Jackson had such a long history together, did Lucius have any knowledge as to what Scott's father might've done in his life to prompt leaving that notebook behind? There was nothing Scott detected from the grizzled lawyer suggesting he knew anything.

The paperwork in question landed in front of Scott and disappeared as fast as it arrived. For a writer, Scott should've taken more time to read the petition, but there was something about Lucius he trusted.

"Do you have any questions for me, Scott?" Lucius asked him. It was fatherly in its own way, making Scott appreciate the man even more.

Scott inhaled and he put out his hand as he rose. "None that I can think of, Lucius. I'll call you if anything comes to mind. Right now, I have two hard days to get through, and after that, I'm mountains-bound to Deep Creek to honor Dad's request."

"Mmm hmm," Lucius said, looking scatterbrained for a moment as he shook Scott's hand for the second time. "His will does stipulate cremation and what he wanted you to do for him thereafter. Very poetic."

"He loved fishing for trout when he could still do it and, when I was much younger, hiking on the Swallow Falls trail. I never really took him too seriously, but he has a designated spot across from the waterfall where I'm supposed to scatter him. He'd proposed to my mother there, that much I know. I haven't been to Deep Creek since I was a kid, but I'll figure it all out. My girlfriend's terrific company and she can blaze a trail like it's her own Spartan race."

"I like it," Lucius said, swinging around his desk with a ginger sway. "Whatever a Spartan race is, anyway."

Lucius led Scott back to the tight quartered lobby. Scott took a second look at the framed Rufus Thomas 45 and for a second, he'd wanted to make small talk about funk and soul music, which Scott loved as much as rock n' roll and its affiliated branches down the line. He dismissed the urge after watching Lucius move at half the pace of Scott, lumbering with all that mass, but keeping a jovial smile upon his face.

At her desk, Tobie was flying her fingers across a keyboard, words floating across an open Word document spread across her monitor. As she was in Lucius' age bracket, Scott marveled at her speed. She was the exact opposite of her boss and generational counterpart.

"You take care now, Mr. Bischoff," Tobie told Scott with a gentle knell matching the gentle swerve of her neck.

"You too, ma'am," Scott returned with a smile, feeling a ridiculous urge to Stax snap his fingers, but having the good sense not to.

"It breaks my heart your father went the way he did," Lucius said with an exaggerated sigh. "We're dying off, one-by-one, my man. Tobie might outlive us all though, dynamo that she is."

"Pshaw," she pretend-scoffed, her thin, rapid fingers keeping true to their task. Scott noticed the absence of any rings on those fingers, versus the eye-catching hardware Lucius sported.

"Again, my condolences to you, Scott," Lucius said, with a rocking to his hip which made Scott feel sad for him. He hoped Lucius' short-lived football career at least carried some glory days to hold onto through his aches and wobbles. "Anything I can do, of course."

"Dad really liked you, Lucius. I can see why, and I forgive you for the divorce."

Lucius held his cumbersome belly as he roared in laughter. Tobie stopped her work long enough to join him and to flash Scott a wiry thumbs-up.

"Jesus, Scott, I know things ended bad between us, but you couldn't have shown enough decency to let me know your father died? If I hadn't called your mom about the deed copy to our old house we'd left with her, I would never have known."

Scott was rubbing his left temple as he held his cell phone a few inches from his right ear. The squawking was enough to shred his suddenly throbbing brain, much less his ear canal. He kept his face turned toward the front window at Kaizoku Poke Bowl, knowing he was being looked at by others in his vicinity. In the back of his mind, he was cursing them all as much as he was cursing Carly under his breath. While he was at it, he threw himself a full litany of vulgarity for taking her call.

Everyone around him seemed way too happy for a workday, even if most of the tables were occupied by patrons who, like himself, appeared to have no intent of giving up their ground for a while. Their nattering was making Scott wish he'd taken his Nabeyaki udon to go. He'd enjoyed meeting Lucius Jackson, but the appointment had nonetheless left Scott with a headache he wasn't shocked had come.

"Maryland land records have free public access online, you know," Scott muttered, leaving all traces of sarcasm coated to his voice. If she could only see his detestation as much as hear it. "Why you needed to bother Mom with this—"

"He was my father-in-law once, you know," Carly throttled him through the phone.

Each clunk inside Scott's head felt like a Lego brick of the brain interlocking itself with another, creating a cubical pile of pain with each loud, obnoxious snap.

"Carly," he droned, continuing to rub his temple. "Who do you think you are? I'm not at home right now, so I can't pull the divorce papers out of the file cabinet. Yet I'm pretty sure there's no hidden clause in our decree mandating I *owe* you any communication. We have no kids; you bailed out on me for the southwest. Let's get real, huh? Would you really have come all the way from Galveston for the funeral? Speaking of which, what the hell time is it over there? You're up too early to be giving me shit. I should talk, having Japanese noodles before 11:00."

"I'm only an hour behind you and *yes,* I would've," Carly fumed. Her tone was growing thicker and madder, only contributing to Scott's thumping. "I can't believe you'd assume otherwise. We're divorced, but we still need to act like adults. I would let you know if something happened to my parents, whether you came to the funeral or not. They liked you and I shouldn't say this, but they still do."

"Car, you couldn't have picked a worse time to start a fight."

"I'm not trying to start a —"

"Though don't think I'm not laughing inside," Scott interrupted. "We've said more in this conversation than the last three years of our marriage."

"That's a cheap shot."

"Yep, and you earned it," Scott said with such rancor he'd lured the stares of two guys with predictable recessions in their hairlines to match their predictable business suits. To them he put up his free hand and made a gabbing gesture, pointing at the phone and rolling his eyes upwards. They both smirked and left Scott be.

"I never wanted things to go the way they did," Carly badgered.

"Yet it was *you* who left *me.* Or do I need to play the whole scene out for all of Cambridge's finest for their entertainment?"

"Scott, I —"

"Oh, Scott *nothing*," he groused. "You want to open old wounds? I'm not interested. All I ever wanted was to be loved, Carly."

"So did I, Scott!"

"I think we both have different concepts of what being loved entails. Maybe Richard can tell me your point of view on the subject these days?"

"Low blow..."

"Cliff's Notes to our final chapter, you found someone who loved kids, even though you and I are both kinda old to be new parents. He was a widower with a built-in nest of adoptees, so you took off together, future destination, Galveston. You two had planned it out, for Christ's sake! How do you think that made me feel?"

"I swear Richard and I never did anything until you and I were separated."

"Big whoop. By the time you'd communicate with me, it was from another man's home, one with three kids already part of the deal. I think that hurt the most, hearing Richard's daughter address you by your name in the background."

"According to your Facebook feed, you're doing just fine for yourself," Carly muttered with clear derision. "She's pretty."

"Christ, I unfriended you ages ago, Car," Scott said, matching her contempt. "Stalker."

"Change your settings to private, then."

"I'll take your advice."

"Well, I guess that's it, then," Carly said with a sigh sounding more than pouty. "I was going to ask if you're doing okay, but it sounds like you have things well in-hand."

"Right now, I have my goddamn head in my hand. Before you called, it was a pair of chopsticks for udon growing cold."

"Okay, well, I don't know when I'll speak to you again, Scott, so I'll wish you luck. Take care."

Carly didn't wait for Scott to respond. He'd heard the click in his ear faster than she'd hung up on him.

As the suits rose from their table, one of them leaned down to Scott.

"That's brutal, brother."

"Like the Kansas song, dust in the wind," Scott returned with a feeble click of a finger gun.

"If you know me, you know my father was a problematic man."

Even though only a handful of people were sitting in front of him, Scott was nervous, as if he'd been forced to deliver a lecture on quantum physics to a capacity full auditorium. Including the priest from St Joseph's, Father Stan Strazinski, who'd led a subdued though strangely beautiful funeral service, there were eleven people in attendance.

Kate wore a tasteful gray, one-piece sleeveless dress. She'd caught a few rays yesterday in an outdoor lunch meeting and her impromptu tan made her toned arms spectacular. Scott's mother, no longer married to the deceased, had chosen a navy blue dress suit with a turquoise blouse. Larry, Scott's surrogate and truest father in all senses of the word, was dressed in conservative beige slacks with a suit jacket matching the azure shade of his wife. Knowing how much Larry despised dressing up, Scott permitted himself a brief smile as he spotted Larry tugging on his blue and maroon striped tie like an eight-year-old boy—with full hatred of the thing.

Amazingly, Scott's cousin Andy had shown, bringing along his wife, Lydia and their four kids, all girls: Constance, Abra, Aileen and Lyric. Andy was the only one of Scott's cousins who'd shown up. Not even his Uncle Gene, having relocated to Fairfax, Virginia, had made the effort to come, much less be bothered to call Scott back after he'd left a message sharing the news of his dad's passing. It appeared a conference was held amongst the contingency of his father's country-scattered kin and Andy had been the designated representative of the entire clan. Andy's bunch had made the trip down from Pittsburgh.

Scott just now noticed only the priest was wearing black. Not even Scott himself, the direct aggrieved. He'd worn gray slacks, a mauve dress shirt and a blazer close in color to his mom's deep blue. No tie. For whatever reason, Scott had hung his necktie selection back up as fast as he'd chosen it. An unspoken form of protest, perhaps.

To his left and surrounded by a few bouquets of flowers was a cobalt urn holding his father's ashes. On an easel stood a three by two board with a handful of pinned pictures which Scott had pulled from his photo albums before his meeting with Lucius Jackson. A few were old shots taken in the days of the Instamatic 104, with the old flash cubes nobody raised in the age of the cell phone camera would remember. Nearly five decades old, the colors were washed gruesomely, but the images were solid enough to show Scott being held as a baby by a slimmer, robust version of his dad. Scott found his mother wiping a tear earlier after looking at that shot.

"I didn't marry no mutt back then," she'd said at the easel with Scott's arm draped around her and Kate rubbing her back. Already his mother had validated Kate, this being their fourth interaction, by telling Scott she was lovely while adjusting his shirt collar in a way only a mother could. Even better, he'd received an on-the-lam thumbs-up of Kate's approval from Larry.

The other tacked pictures showed Scott's father at work on his model railroading layout, his great passion in life. One showed him holding up B&O and Colorado & Western line engines and one had him dragging a sculptor's blade along the surface of an in-progress mountain incline. All of which had been abandoned then donated to a local firehouse for their Christmas diorama as Scott's dad grew older. The last photo Scott had selected depicted his father holding a plaque commemorating 40 years of service with the Social Security Administration, only a few years before his old man had taken his retirement.

"I wish I could fill your ears with great stories about my dad," Scott continued, "but I'm not going to sugarcoat anything. My nights as a child were spent listening to open range combat between my parents. Dad was a heavy drinker, so he wasn't much of a conversationalist to me, except to criticize me when I couldn't do a math problem, drank my Tang too fast, spilled the milk or if I had a grass stain on my jeans. For my mother, he had few words as well, but when he did speak to her, it was usually in anger. After a while, the fights just started bleeding into one another, and they became a nighttime ritual. My official bedtime back then was 8:00, but the fights would keep me up past ten many times. I had an advanced tutorial in profanity but was smart enough never to use it in school...through fifth grade, anyway."

The laughter he received would've been considered faint from a normal crowd. With so few people and a lot of empty chairs provided by Briggs Funerary Services, it was amplified and given soundtrack by a milky sounding organ through the overhead speaker. "I Know That My Redeemer Lives" thus came off squelchy instead of uplifting.

"Dad and I butted heads a lot," Scott continued. "I wanted to be a writer. He wanted me to be a numbers cruncher. I'm a dreamer, he was a pragmatist. I despise politics; he thought the world revolved around Capitol Hill. He was never open to trying new things. He was set in his ways."

Scott saw his mother nod at that.

"I'll stop the hate parade there because I'll end up keeping us here longer than anyone needs this morning. My girlfriend Kate's been my counsel to hear all the stories and my mom lived a good deal of them with me, so I'll spare the rest of you. What I can say is there was a time after the divorce, when my dad was actually cool. He would take me to the Orioles games a lot, and I got to worship Eddie Murray, Lee May and Al Bumbry at the church of Memorial Stadium, forgive me, Father. I saw many miracles on 33rd Street."

Father Stan gave him a wave of dismissal with a gentle laugh.

"My father was complicated, combustive and at times, an outright pain in the ass, excuse my language. If I regret anything, it's letting his quirks, eccentricities, and mean-spiritedness drive me away sometimes. I probably could've done better by him the older and weirder he got. A fault of mine is I despise drama and conflict. Sixth grade did that to me, and well, so did the years my mother and father had their problems. I'm happy to say they resolved their differences later in life for my sake, and I appreciate their efforts. Dad was a guy who'd shut himself off from the world and got his news from the paper instead of the tv. Being a newspaper reporter myself, I liked that about him, even if I had to bring him copies of my work. He was a *News American* guy to the bitter end. Though he routinely antagonized his neighbors, I'm happy to see through the viewings he touched *some* people in the right way. For the good times, Dad, thanks. I love you."

There'd been no reception after the service, only hugs in parting and promises exchanged been Scott and Andy's family to get together sometime for a family gathering which he doubted would ever occur. Andy had whispered to Scott, "She's a knockout," referring to Kate. "I'm pulling for you, bud." On the nearer horizon, Scott's mom and Larry invited him and Kate over for Sunday dinner in a couple weeks.

That night, Kate made grilled salmon at her condo, doused with a mixture of soy and wasabi sauces. She served it overtop spinach leaves and added asparagus, pan seared in hollandaise, for the side. She broke open some Riesling as she and Scott took down more than half the bottle with Scott getting the heavier pour. They ate in silence for a few minutes as Scott sagged at his plate while carving off portions of the tender salmon with his fork. For a few moments, he had reservations drinking the wine.

You're not him, Scott growled at himself, pulling on his wine glass and licking the residue from his upper lip. *Not like that plaster saint you'll be taking up to Deep Creek.*

At Scott's insistence, Kate went to work after the funeral. She was rolling through the events of her day, dropping marketing lingo Scott only knew by basic meaning instead of through hands-on application like "action alley," "tear sheets" and "flighting." The latter, Kate spent the most time talking about, given one of her clients' dissatisfactions with her firm. A statewide dental practice chain, Underwood Family Dentistry was losing business to a private dentistry a county away in Cardin Bluffs, prompting an abrupt cutoff of their high-impact advertising. Kate herself had spearheaded the campaign and Kate herself took the chew-out.

Though Scott kept his ear as attentive as he could, he barely heard Kate grumble, "They're a bunch of pissants anyway," citing her liaison, Bill something-or-other at Underwood, had threatened to move the account to The Anders Group's biggest competitor, Rogers Boutique Marketing Firm. Rogers was where, Kate claimed, the testosterone count well outnumbered the estrogen. Their ops played accordingly.

"Wow, that sucks," Scott drolled in response to Kate's report.

Kate then changed subjects, mentioning she'd scored her wasabi salmon recipe via a free sample at Asia-Plus Mart, joking the two of them could enjoy enough storewide handouts on a given weekend to make it a cheap date. "I'm not sure how cost effective the store's method is since the sample portions are generous, but being in marketing by trade, it certainly works on *me*."

They cleared, washed, and dried the dishes together, though Scott said very little as they worked efficiently.

"I know you're hurting, but did I do something wrong?" Kate asked, stopping Scott in mid-motion. She grabbed the damp drying towel from him and slung it overtop her shoulder.

"No," Scott answered, putting on a smile he didn't quite feel up to. "Dinner was amazing, the wine was amazing. *You*....you're amazing. It's just the finality of it all, you know. My dad. I kept looking at the urn all day and well, it's official; he's never coming back."

"I know," Kate said, throwing her arms around Scott's neck. "I also know you're dealing with finding your father the way you did. If I could buy you a memory wipe of it, I'd pay any price."

"He wasn't the greatest dad by any stretch, but nobody deserves to die like that."

"He lived alone by choice, Scott. As you've told me many times already, he was never going to move, no matter how many times you tried to steer him towards a senior community. This was bound to happen. You can't blame yourself."

"I tried like hell to help him, but he refused every single time," Scott sighed, pulling Kate closer to him and resting his chin on her shoulder. "I feel like I should've done more."

"I can't walk in your shoes," Kate moaned, planting her hand on Scott's cheek, "but I have my own pain and regrets. All my family relocated to Montana, and don't think I wasn't made to feel guilty for staying here in Maryland. I have more than a job here; it's a career. I love what I do and I get a respectable salary for it. My father can be ruthless when he wants to be, and he's claimed more than once I've abandoned everyone when, in fact, *they're* the ones who packed up and rolled out. To an extent, I understand the misguided guilt you're feeling. You can't absorb the brunt for your father's choices any more than I can, though. Does that make sense?"

"Perfect. Funny enough, I'm a writer and there's a thousand things I want to say, but nothing comes out. Scott Secret, I'm afraid of what's in that notebook."

"Kate Confidential, I'm more afraid of what *you're* going to do more than what's in the notebook."

When they retired to Kate's bedroom, she vanished into her master bathroom to freshen herself. She returned wearing nothing but a jasmine scent from Sephora which Scott had raved on in the past.

"Alright, lover, let me take your mind away for..."

Kate shook her head, feeling the spontaneous broil inside of her smolder.

Scott hadn't even gotten out of his clothes, oblivious to her nudity and everything else around him.

"Poor guy," she whispered, kissing him on the forehead then pulling off his shoes. She turned out the light and wrapped herself around Scott, taking comfort in the steady but protracted rise and fall of his chest beneath her palm. "Kate Confidential, I think I love you."

The next morning, Scott received a call from his editor at the *Baldwin Hills Times*.

"Hey, Sam," Scott said at a low volume. He was already being drowned out by Kate's hair dryer close by in her master bath.

"Hey, Scottie, how's it going?" Sam said, raising his voice over the competition. It made Scott wince, but he didn't say anything about it. "I'm sorry I didn't come by to pay my respects. Deadlines, you know what I'm up against."

"Don't worry about it, man. The flowers were appreciated."

"Least we could do. So look, I know you're still getting over your father and all, but Russ Hicklin called. Says he emailed you the other day and never heard back. I explained your situation."

"Russ is a friend of the press, but if you don't answer him right away...yeah, I get it. Sorry, Sam, I haven't been checking my email the past couple of days. You understand."

"I do, and Randi Sommers did a fine job covering for you the other day. Turned in a clean, professional piece. I never worry about her, but Russ, you know how the good ol' boy network operates."

"Right. He once told me on the record he still has a problem addressing Janette Stevens and Mary Frank as council*women*. I never printed that, of course."

"Sounds like a pig!" Kate shouted from the bathroom in between the noticeable sound of brushing and the tugging of twined hair clusters, followed by her double grunts of "Ow!"

Scott smirked at her, catching only a glimpse of her tight burgundy skirt which hugged her thigh and stopped at the knee. Here in Kate's condo, she moved even faster getting ready for work than she did at his house. No matter where they'd slept, however, she'd insisted on immediate tooth brushing before any good morning kisses. He'd collected a palette of Crest and a juicy smacker only minutes before Sam called him.

"Well, he trusts *you*, not Randi," Sam dragged on. "I'm sorry if this is adding more pressure than you need this week, but he wants you to reach out to him. Summer's almost over, but you know the town's been on strict water regs most of the summer. Earl Scaggs was handed a citation last week for washing his car, but what really has folks riled up is old Mrs. Bennett. She was cited for watering her flower bed. Everyone knows that sweet but senile bird is the furthest thing from a law breaker. Served on the Jaycee auxiliary forever until she retired. Russ wants you to take his statements and help try to do some damage control. Sooner than later, natch."

"I get you, Sam," Scott heaved into the phone.

"But I'm getting you at a bad time."

"Yeah, but I can get over myself."

"That's not what I mean, Scott. Hey, I heard a woman's voice a moment ago. Are you seeing someone?"

"Yeah," Scott said with a bashful grin only he could see reflected in Kate's vanity mirror across from her bed. "I'll introduce her sometime."

"Thank God, *finally* you can put Carly to rest. She never was the right one for you. Look, Scottie, I can take Russ' statements myself if you like, but I'm going to need your word magic. Sorry to be a cold-hearted bastard, but please reach out to Russ, then hit me up and we'll figure out a game plan for this...whatever you want to call it."

"A saving face editorial by the town planner."

"Couldn't have glorified it better," Sam said with a laugh. "Be safe. If you need anything, holler."

"Thanks, Sam, I'll be fine."

Thinking about the notebook, which he couldn't put off any longer, Scott was the furthest thing from fine.

"Are you sure you don't want to wait another day or two, babe?"

They were back at Scott's place for the night. Kate's overnight bag and groceries hadn't even made it past the foyer before they'd made love right on the steps leading upstairs. This being a midlife renewal, they'd joked while taking a shower together afterwards how they wished *AARP* magazine had its own version of *Penthouse Forum,* just to brag.

After reheating the bag of fried chicken Kate had brought with her and heating up a can of green beans, they'd settled in Scott's living room. He was in a pair of black boxer briefs with red piping and a Baltimore Orioles t-shirt. Kate wore nothing but Scott's oversized, pine-colored terrycloth robe. She was drowned in the thing and overtly pleased by it.

"Let's do this while the effects of the past hour are still with me. Scott Secret, that was the best sex I've had in decades."

"Kate Confidential," she cooed back, squirming inside the robe until she could loosen her bare leg to drag up Scott's. "You'd better keep working out and boosting your cardio, because you ain't seen nothing yet."

"Hurt me," Scott teased, pulling the notebook up with his right hand. It still stunk, but he was in too good a mood to care. His left grabbed Kate's ankle and planted it across his lap.

He skimmed past the little he'd already read, then picked up from there, this time reading aloud for Kate's benefit:

Before I get into the hard part, I want to say, Scott, I regret everything I put you and your mother through. I know you don't believe me, but I hope you will one day.

This may sound trite after all these years, but I know how badly I screwed up. No woman ever stood up to me the way your mother did. I respected her, more than either of you could imagine. We fought like enemies and I wish we hadn't. What you had to listen to back then, it's kept me up at night sometimes. For my part, I am terribly sorry.

I've said the same to your mother and we've stayed amicable towards each other all these years because of it. I've done her dirty in the past, but if there's one thing I've done right in my life, it's mending fences with her. We did it for your sake, but the guilt I feel even today knowing I messed up, well, that part was so I could go to the grave one day knowing I'd made things right with your mother.

"No grave to be had, old man," Scott said, glancing over his father's ashes in the urn sitting on a lamp table across from them. Scott hadn't bothered turning the lamp itself on.

Kate kept quiet and her hands tucked deep into the sleeves of the robe.

I know how much damage I've caused. I know there's a part of you that still hates me, and I've earned that. If you're reading this now, you must be either at Deep Creek or soon on your way, because I know you have honor and I know whatever anger you still have towards me, it's not enough to deny me my final wish. I love you for your courage, son. God knows I should've done better for you.

Larry has been such a blessing to you, Scott. He did what I didn't have the conviction to do, to be there for you every day, to be a parent no matter how good or bad the experiences were, and I know there was plenty of both. I love Larry as much as the rest of you. I can be man enough to admit you would not be the fine person you are today without him.

Now, with all the mushy stuff out of the way, I don't know how you're going to take any of what I have to say next. It will change your life. It will almost certainly change your perception of me, and I know how terrible that already must be. Whatever enmity you have towards me now, that's likely to grow and I accept that, even if I know in my heart I should've had the stones to tell you all of this to your face.

If you think me a coward after reading this, I'll understand. You deserve better than this handwritten account, but I am acting in accordance with the events that happened. It's also been in protection of another person, someone I love as much as your mother. Your mom already knows what I'm about to tell you.

"Whaaaaaat?" Kate whispered.

What I hope, Scott, is that by coming clean about this, you might find the good in it, for your own future. This is so hard, son.

I know I've lived as a hermit, for lack of a better term, Scott read on before Kate stopped him again.

"A whining hermit, you mean," she scoffed. "Jesus, Scott, I'm kinda glad I never met him."

"I don't blame you," Scott said, feeling his chest fill with anxiety as his breathing increased with anticipation. An hour ago, it had done the same thing with a far more satisfying outcome.

I want you to have some sort of peace of mind there was more to my life than you know. Your mother and I worked hard to cover it up and I don't want to undo her good intentions.

You know I was unfaithful to your mother once, but that's about all we've discussed. I am so sorry I did that to her. Then again, to deny my affair would mean denying you even exist.

"Oh, dear God," Kate gasped, trembling as much as Scott was right now. She could feel sweat growing between his usually sturdy hand and her ankle. A spasm down Scott's arm and into his palm quaked between them. She didn't need to see his skin flush red to know his blood pressure was rising. "Scott, put it down. Don't read anymore."

"I can't *not* read it," he quivered, continuing on.

Well, I've delayed all I can with this rambling, so I'll get on with it.

I'm a cheater, a drunk, a chain smoker, and a hothead. As the younger people say today, I own it...all of it.

Her name is Bonnie. She's your biological mother.

"That unbelievable bastard," Kate said as loud as she dared, pulling her leg back and tucking it under the folds of the robe before shifting position to wrap her arms around Scott and squeeze him with of her worth.

"Jesus, Dad," Scott said in a numb voice, letting his head ease into the nook of Kate's shoulder. "Why couldn't you have told me while you were alive?"

"He was a goddamn weakling, that's why," Kate hissed, glancing at the urn. "Oh, Scott, I'm so sorry. Put the book down and let me hold you."

"Not yet, there's more," Scott said.

"More?" she asked, releasing him.

"Yeah, listen..."

Bonnie was in no financial condition to raise you, Scott.

"She sucks," Kate interrupted again.

Your mother's a remarkable woman and I'll always love her for taking you as her own child. We kept it quiet from you, but we went through the adoption process to allow your mother to have legal custody with me. After the divorce, she got you full-time with my having weekend visitations. I'll never be able to repay the debt of kindness that woman showed me. Showed you.

I know how rotten I've been to you at times. Don't think it didn't hurt for me to hear you say to Carly my problems are from my living alone. I looked up Bonnie years later and we picked up where we'd left off, maintaining our separate homes and lives, but seeing each other on and off until she died in 1998 of an aneurysm. Since then, I've had no other woman. I lost the two I'll ever love and I have to live with the shame of what I've done. I can only hope to ease any pain you're feeling by setting the record straight.

I love you, Scott, and I'm so proud of you.

    Dad

That weekend, Scott and Kate took a three-hour drive into Western Maryland. They'd rented a one-bedroom cabin spotted a convenient mile away from the lower entrance into the Swallow Falls trail. From his youth, Scott remembered it had been considered a locals' trail and he was happy all these years later to see that fact remained. The tourists went the extra two miles up north toward the top of the falls system.

Scott had turned in his copy about the town water ban to Sam on Thursday night before it went to press the following day. Sam had complimented the tightness of the piece. He'd also shot Scott a couple of emails from female readers who'd praised Scott and issued their support of their fellow townies while bashing their elected town planner. The word "chauvinist" in the same sentence as Russ Stricklin's name had appeared in both messages. Scott and Kate joked about it on the road and again during a quick stop for turkey avocado sandwiches and Glaceau vitamin water.

"I'm glad the few people we've come across out here haven't said anything about the urn," Scott said, keeping the edge out of his voice. He was feeling nervous, and not just because of the task he was set to.

"As long as it's not a park ranger, we should be fine," Kate said, glancing around the woods anyway. "Take it easy, inhale the pristine air around us. This is more than your father deserves, but I don't fault his aesthetics."

"The saving grace is Mom was relieved when I called to tell her I knew the truth about Bonnie. When I told her it changed nothing between us, that she'll always be my mother no matter what, I know it gave her peace. Seriously, Kate, I just can't get my head around some other woman I've never known, nor will I get the chance to."

"Persona non grata as far I'm concerned," Kate said, hooking her forefinger into the rear belt loop of Scott's Levis as they tramped over jutting rocks and crunched down castaway branches on the path. The aroma from the bellowing rapids in the river filled the air around them, sending a far-flung mist to lick their skin.

When they found the spot Scott figured was the right one judging by the roar of the falls, he pointed it out to Kate, then put his arm around her. Seeing nobody around, they descended the rocky slope leading to the fall's plunge pool.

"Worth the trip," Kate said in awe, nudging Scott's hip with her own. "Especially making a whole weekend of it together."

"Unplugged, no less. How are you going to get along without wi-fi access, babe?"

"Open the Jameson bottle later on the cabin porch; you might get a whole slew of Kate Confidentials out of me."

"My first Scott Secret of the trip is my dad may have been a hot mess, but he would've loved you."

"Hmm, nice thought under the circumstances. Do you have any words you want to say for him?"

"Thanks for putting me with the right woman to be my mom," Scott said aloud, detaching from Kate and unscrewing the urn. "May you find Bonnie again and have a blast of a reset like we will in the cabin later."

"Here's to resets," Kate said, pecking Scott on the cheek.

Comic Con

"SO WHAT'S IT ABOUT?"

I take a deep breath, glancing down at the retro red and white checkerboard Vans loafers of the young guy leafing through my comic book. I had those same loafers once, back in '84. We used to say "rad" and "gnarly" a lot then. It was the year Alan Moore took over *Swamp Thing*. Kevin Eastman and Peter Laird debuted *Teenage Mutant Ninja Turtles*. The Teen Titans (not the wisecracking Cartoon Network caricatures) and Power Pack were big hits, but most notably, Spiderman went black in *Amazing Spidey* #252 after returning from the Secret Wars. The alien symbiote costume affixed to Peter Parker would change the imprint's dynamic forever. If you're into comic books, Venom needs no further introduction.

The kid wasn't really reading my words, nor taking too deep a glance at my creative partner, Stefan Günter's art. Stefan's lettering chops are just as much to brag about, on par with anyone assigned to the likes of Tom King, Geoff Johns, Jason Aaron, Kelly Thompson, Amy Chu, Greg Pak, Chip Zdarsky or Kelly Sue DeConnick, all of whom were on hand to sign their best-selling comics at the Richmond Comic Con.

To even mention those professionals in the same context as me or Stefan is sheer presumptuousness, but when you have your own product to hype, you must act like you've been touring the national con circuit instead of haunting a local comic caucus only.

I've spent three hours now pushing free copies of my debut comic,

Nuke Boy, and things could be going better. I came with a 250-print run, 248 after giving my boys their own copies. To the good, Stan Sakai accepted one before autographing and without prompt or a commission fee, doodling the head of his signature samurai rabbit, Miyamoto Usagi, on my first print copy of *Albedo Anthropomorphics* #2. It marks the first appearance of *Usagi Yojimbo.* A sweet man, Mr. Sakai. That alone paid for my $34.95 admission fee.

"The art's *meh,*" the kid tells me with all the privilege he feels like grabbing from an entire scene built on fan self-entitlement. He takes a nonobligatory preview like most readers do Wednesdays at their local comic shops on new release day. When you've crossed into your forties, much less fifties like me; anyone ten years behind you ranks as a kid, and this guy's a greenhorn in college if there ever was one. I mean, just look at the dead craters on his face saying he may be done with Oxy washes, or they could strike back with an act of vengeance even the folks at Marvel might cringe at. The *Resident Evil* ball cap and *Rick and Morty* shirt says it all about the kid. In my day, if someone handed you a freebie book at a gathering like this, you had enough common courtesy to say "Thank you," even if you passed it on to a friend after reading it.

"It's free, dude," I tell him, pivoting with a copy of *Nuke Boy* #1 in my hand, thrusted out to a graying, wrinkled, porker of a man who could call *me* a kid. He's dressed in a Bane t-shirt, illustrated by Kelley Jones. From the game-changing *Knightfall* storyline running through *Batman* and *Detective Comics* in 1993 and '94. That much, I like about him. The bristly, aged ponytail, the tent-sized cargo shorts flapping around his knees and the shameless collision of tube socks and sandals has me thinking of Comic Book Guy from *The Simpsons.* Worst geriatric ensemble ever. He's lugging a stuffed bag of comics and he has a boxed Harley Quinn statuette (classic Harley, not the gangbanger hot shorts version) tucked beneath his unwieldly armpit. Just as cocky as his animated likeness, the guy sneers at my comic and moves on without comment. He had an open hand, for Christ's sake.

"Yeah, I can see why," the pimple casualty says to me with the same dismissiveness. "Your boy, Stefan whatever, he wishes he was Fiona Staples. Nowhere in the same league. Pass."

He hands me back the comic and takes off.

By my estimation, I've passed out less than half of my copies, already getting tired of the rejection treatment to a costless comic.

I may not be as high profile as Free Comic Book Day the first Saturdays of each May, but the fickleness of the fans makes me wonder if I'm in over my head. I try to picture what resistance Dave Sim might've run into hawking *Cerebus* during the late Seventies. Or Matt Fraction with *Sex Criminals* before its release in 2013.

I've managed to give out *Nuke Boy* #1 to the Dynamite, Image, Boom! Studios, and Dark Horse booths and a few of the indie prints. I engaged and collected business cards with the reps on hand at their tables. A big step up from my *Star Wars* trading card days where I could be just as personable and shrewd in swapping my two-for-one doubles for singles I needed. I had fun talking to the president of Publishing and Marketing of Boom! Studios after attending their panel earlier. He liked that I owned their six-issue miniseries from 2014, *Six-Gun Gorilla.*

It's the con attendees who are the harder sell. We're all here in celebration of the medium and to embrace our open license to shine our geekery like football and soccer fans and their replica jerseys and team color warpaint. Getting some DIY love around here, though, it's nowhere easier than breaking in an upstart gridiron league against the NFL.

The people who've stopped to look at my book, some kept. The others scrutinize *Nuke Boy* as they might a new X-Men miniseries featuring a team of unheard-of mutants spearheaded by only one familiar legacy hero. Sad fact, untested books from independent publishers are dissected with even more brutality than crossover epic yarns from The Big Two. As in Marvel or DC, who control most of the shelf space and also the profit in this industry. The Coke and Pepsi of the genre.

I drown out the echoing drone and the loudspeaker MC announcing the arrival of David Mazouz, the teen Bruce Wayne from Fox's *Gotham* tv series because it annoys me. Those who purchased meet-and-greet passes with David have been invited to head over for their autograph and photo op session with Batman-to-be. I'm kinda jealous because I spent a ton on the print run of *Nuke Boy,* which meant I couldn't spring for the convention amenities. Bad enough I'm rolling around without a business card. I'm positive half of my declines by the publishers is because I'm not sticking contact cards inside my courtesy copies. Forget Comic Book Man; I'm feeling more like Homer Simpson himself. Throw a blustering word balloon overhead to accompany me the rest of the con and rain my shame upon me: "DOH!"

I'm about to give up, because it's dawning on me one of the biggest things going against me aside from no business cards is the unspoken edict that free reeks of desperation. However, luck hits me with the next person coming by.

He's carrying all eight trade paperbacks collecting James Tynion, IV's run of *The Woods.* Unlike many of the conventioneers, he's not wearing any comics' couture or anything more flamboyant beyond a rainbow patterned Pride wristband I spot peeking from beneath the cuff of his powder blue dress shirt. He's tucked in and his khaki pants are pressed so tight you can see the ridges slicing down each front leg. He might have come to the Richmond Comic Con right out of a hair salon. His salt and pepper hair is crisp and it smells pleasing, like it had been sprayed with lilac. His mustache and beard have been meticulously trimmed. He stands out like a reformer in this den of geeks.

"How's it going?" I try him, hoping to avoid sounding like I'd give my left ball sac for just one read. Of a freebie, no less. Something tells me to switch up my pitch a little. "I'm Denny Crowley. Would you be open to reading a promotional copy of a brand-new comic series under the Shred Comix imprint, *Nuke Boy?*"

Before he answers, the guy scans me before the book. I can feel the onyx in his eyes running all over my sides and around my face. I haven't had a date in weeks, though it's the female genus I'm after. I'm flattered, kinda-sorta, but I'm also feeling grimy and unworthy once the guy tilts his head away after he's evaluated me. I'm not his type. I'd taken it far worse when Jeanine Severino did the same exact thing to me back in high school after I'd asked her to Prom.

"Sure," he says, holding out his open hand to receive a copy of the comic. I congratulate myself. The changeup in delivery has paid off. "Tell me what it's about."

"So check it," I tell him through my throat, which has gone parched. Maybe a good thing, because I've already undone my professionalism with my stupid, untroubled intro spiel. My tongue now feels like I'd been licking the microfibers on the sleeve of my Mister Miracle shirt all afternoon. I'm craving a Gatorade from one of the vending machines in the tucked-away cafeteria in the east wing of the subterranean convention floor. Blue Ice. I can taste it like I can the lard in the crinkle fries they serve here, but I want a readership more than I want to kvetch in silence over thirst.

"Okay," he says, waiting on me to get going. Just by the mere prompt, the man (who hasn't given me his name, nor do I expect him to) lingers on Stefan's splash cover. A good sign. I hope the sight of a teenager plowing toward the reader on a skateboard in a war-torn hellhole being chased by a gaggle of cops-turned-wasteland punkers ala *The Road Warrior* and a prefiguring nuclear cloud behind it all entices him to keep it.

"It's a dystopian action series," I say to my potential reader, getting back into marketing mode. I have to compete with James Tynion, IV, one of the elite writers of the scene. Seems like Tynion's everywhere a comic book is these days, Gotham City, The Hall of Justice, a town cursed by human-gorging aliens, a high school of the damned, a Frank Lloyd Wright-esque villa with no escape from the gates of the apocalypse. I feel miniscule by comparison.

"Alright," the man says, and I can see by his eyes he not only wants to hear more, he wants me to be quicker about it. I let it sieve from that point.

"My protagonist is a skater teen, Trey, fending for himself and his pregnant teen sister in a holocaust striking the outer rim of Washington, DC. The superpowers have finally nuked each other. Forget zombies, though...my name's not Romero nor Kirkman."

"Alright," he repeats himself, though I'm the opposite of discouraged when he adds, "My only concern is this being derivative of *Tank Girl*."

"One of my all-time favorite titles," I shove with confidence. "I go nowhere near it, though. My book is more serious, and its set in America, not the UK. No flatulence, boob flashes or balling kangaroo hybrids, either."

He laughs, another good sign.

"It's not political, is it?" he asks, waggling the comic. I can see he might open it up if he would only set down his Tynion trade paperbacks. "We need more proselytizing in comics like we need straight couple romances. Also, if you have a bunch of technobabble, tell me now and save us both the time. I hate comics that make me feel like I need post-graduate classes in biochemistry, A.I., or forensics. They have their place if the story justifies it, but most of the time, it's all wanking."

"There's something to be said for the classic smash and mash," I say, testing the waters. I have a discerning reader in front of me, but something tells me there's more old school to him than his seasoned mane.

"Bronze Age is where it's at," the guy says, and from his mouth it sounds like the gospel.

"I'd say this is more splatter punk without the psychic warfare of *Akira.* Lawlessness prevails and police protection comes only with material— and sometimes physical—exchange for services, both of which have been depleted from the nuclear fallout."

"A lot of sex, then?" he asks, catching me off-guard.

"Read and find out," I bait him, staying in the pocket. "Anyway, Trey gets around on an old Nuke Boy skateboard which once belonged to his missing father. A relic board from the days of The Germs and Black Flag. You like punk rock?"

"Not really," is the answer I get with no indication as to his music tastes. I don't let it deter me. I'm in the zone despite my growing parch. At this point, I'm just trying to deliver a proposal without a lot of croaking. All this huckstering to move a free book.

"Trey's not only a great boarder like his dad, he can whup your tail with the thing. Faced with the awkward stakes of becoming an uncle in a world no child should be born into, Trey will become an unwitting leader of resistance in my story."

"What's your vision for story length?" he asks, and a part of me cowers. This is a lot of interrogation to pitch a pass-off. I know such elaboration will be expected if I ever want to truly break in, so I keep a poker face on and give him an answer off-the-cuff. To be honest, I never really thought about how long *Nuke Boy* will go, if it even finds an audience.

"I wrote five scripts," I tell him. "I've pictured this as a miniseries with a cliffhanger ending. I'm playing it on the safe side to see if readership warrants keeping it going beyond that."

"You sold me," he says, letting his seeming guard down to laugh at his own joke. "I'll give it a read. Good luck to you, Denny Crowley. I like the shirt, by the way. Kirby forever."

"Appreciate it," I respond, exhaling as he slides *Nuke Boy* on top of his trades. About the only time I expect to one-up James Tynion, IV in this life.

I'm suddenly excited in the same way as when my parents dropped my very first comic book, *Captain America* #201 into my Rolo-smeared mitts at the age of eight. It was the bicentennial year, Spirit of '76. Speaking of Jack Kirby, it was his return to the title. Indeed, Kirby forever.

My pocket buzzes. It's a text from Stefan.

How's the con going, mein freund? Passing out books? Making any connections?

Stefan Günter, Germany's next wunderkind comics artist (as far as I'm concerned, despite the rude critique earlier) is nearly four thousand miles away in Kiel. Thanks to the internet and his near-affluent English, we've bridged a transatlantic collaboration that would never have worked three decades ago.

We email each other files and discuss the plot and storyboards over instant message or Skype. We exchange production costs through PayYou.net. An entertainment lawyer might balk at it, but we have a verbal and signed agreement in .pdf under our joint publication start-up, Shred Comix. We're 50/50 partners on paper, but because Stefan absorbs the harder job as penciller, inker, letterer and colorist, he gets an extra ten percent.

Hell, it's not like we've made any real money yet, though Stefan recouped our initial layout by blasting out his own 250 copy print run at a comic convention in Stuttgart. He *sold* his run, plus he did a pencil commission recreating the cover of *Nuke Boy* #1 for a patron. Even with the Euro conversion, we're in the black by 23 American bucks.

I find another random person, a girl this time. She has a few sex-crazed losers stalking the swish of her blue skirt and the bounce inside of her swabbie-styled white button down and a tied red handkerchief. She's got it swung higher, more like a Freddie Jones ascot. She's shocked her hair pink and she's got a ton of makeup all over her face, including mascara crushed, extended eyelids. However she managed it, her pupils are monstrous, cartoonish-like. I know what she's done. It's a new fad in both the dweeb and erotica undergrounds, girls making themselves look like living, breathing Japanese anime. I hear some are doing it to be a circle jerk target in a real-world version of bukkake. All of this grosses me out.

"Realistic cosplay," I tell her nonetheless, holding out a copy of *Nuke Boy.* "Free comic?"

"No," she says in a frigid tone and the way she looks at me with those flared up eyes, I'm suddenly terrified. I don't care I've failed after reverting to my ill-fated slacker pitch. The sooner this Haifuri wannabe moves on, the better. I may never stream *One Punch Man* again.

Behind them comes a mixed group of guys and girls dressed as the Justice League. "Aquaman" is tricked out as the hunky, long-haired and bearded surfer brah rendition reinvented by Jason Mamoa instead of the archetype blond Charles Atlas King of the Sea version. "Superman" struts his shit since his costume is the shiniest thing on the floor, a perfect facsimile of Henry Cavill, even with his gelled black hair so compact no chunk of Kryptonite could undo it. A brunette "Wonder Woman" rocks the house with a less-metallic gladiator skirt swishing around her; she still radiates as much beauty and butt-kickery as Gal Gadot herself. Her mock golden lasso is merely a yellow rope from a hardware store, but what has everyone laughing, pointing and snapping their picture is the lasso being tied around "The Flash." The red suit and winged headgear is filled out by a teen black girl who's eating the whole domination bit up.

I join the crowd and take a picture of them with my cell before texting it to Stefan, then my boys. I send Stefan a quick message afterwards:

My mouth is tired from the hard sell. A few publishers took a copy and listened to my spiel without ever opening it. Getting regular fans to take a free copy is a bigger fight than Amanda Connor's autograph line. I'll call it cautious optimism.

Stefan must have been waiting on my response as my phone buzzes right away with a one-word response in German: *"Geil!"*

"Awesome," I say aloud, as if Stefan was present to hear my translation. Nobody does hear me, save for a tyke in an oversized Miles Morales Spiderman shirt swooshing around his little knees. I can't imagine what he's thinking in reaction to my voice standing out amidst all the nerdy echo bombs from his tiny height.

After another turndown by a Hispanic couple dressed in Wonder Twin purple leotards with yellow Z on his chest, a corresponding J on hers, I tell myself to deactivate and go get that Gatorade nagging on my mind.

Given her upswing in popularity and what she stands for to a new generation, I see several Captain Marvel cosplayers of varying shapes, and those women stroll the convention hall as proudly as Brie Larsen. They pose with other con attendees for selfies and point their imaginary photon energy blasts at anyone dressed as a Skrull, pealing "Pew! Pew!" in their hilarious, tinny voices.

It feels good to be here without my kids, truth be told. In Comic Cons past, I'd lose half the day parked at Lego vendor tables. The boys balked at my leaving them behind this year, but when I showed Nick and Sean *Nuke Boy* #1, they finally got it. This after years of guilt-tripping me for spending so much of my free time in front of a computer writing. Their mother had left me over it.

The boys said they would brag about my book to their friends, which didn't happen, of course. Nick's copy got crunched beneath his stack of Minecraft manuals. Sean didn't look where he'd put his Hi-C, which got kicked over by Nick's upraised foot in a spastic, angry reaction to getting vaporized in *Fortnite*. Talk to a professional comic book grader what liquid meeting paper does to its value. Or a parent meeting a pissy video game addict's controller.

While I'm standing there pulling on my blue thirst quencher, I hold a copy of my book out, just to see if the minimalist approach could work. Funny enough, it does. My latest taker is some guy shambling more than walking, and he's carrying a replica of the Goth seraph Death from the *Sandman* comics so tight against himself I wonder if he's thinking about doing perverted things to her at home. I can tell he's had black coffee, not only by the empty Dunkin' Donuts cup he's toting around, but by his filmy teeth and the brown splotch above his flabby pectoral. His Judge Dredd tee looks vintage, as it does stretched out, making it even more tragic. He takes *Nuke Boy* through the pinch of two fingers from his coffee hand.

In the flash of a parsec, I feel my bladder take a cheap shot at me. I'd chugged the Gatorade like it was my last shot at it and it ran straight through.

The line for the urinals is as bad as at a summer pavilion concert, but I spot an open stall with nobody in queue. I've been carrying my extra copies of *Nuke Boy* inside a briefcase from an old job I worked at downtown years ago. It was a post-compliance position at Fidelity of Richmond in their retail lending division. I looked almost as silly lugging a briefcase there as I do now at a comic book convention.

I go to wash my hands and I spot, inside the trash can nearby, a copy of *Nuke Boy* #1. It's a kick in the nuts from an invisible comic snob, one who no doubt reads *The Divine and the Wicked* and *Faithless* (as do I) while farting in the general direction of The Avengers.

"Thanks a lot, shmuck," I say out loud, ignoring the stares around me. It's resting on the top of a pile of discarded paper towels, as if left there within the past few minutes. Who was the offending party, anyway? I'm so angry I'm regressing in my head to the tacit kid rule of yesteryear, "No givebacks."

Without shame, I reach down and grab the comic out of the trash and tuck it beneath my signed *Albedo Anthropomorphics* book. I'll tuck both into my briefcase when I get to a more open spot. Then I'll get the hell out of here.

Some flake leaving past me at the trash can mumbles, "Dumpster diver."

"Bite me," I mumble back as I leave the men's room a lot slower than I arrived.

With the sound of guest personality Jess Q. Harnell peeling off one of his hilarious exclamations of "Faboo!" in the key of Wakko Warner from *Animaniacs* over the intercom, I can only muster a smile. Much as I see delighted faces around me in recognition of the character overtop their *zap-biff-boffed* noodles, I feel conquered, as if Doctor Doom dropped a bomb on me. Using a Doombot from a Doom Jet, no less.

I start counting the number of copies I have left inside the brief case and take even more stringent inventory of my bank ledger, flinching at the cost to print them. I'd felt elated for a moment. Now I feel more torn apart than Marc Spector's copious Moon Knight personae. I'm ready to go, tucking my nuked boy ass between my shell-shocked legs.

"Denny Crowley," I hear to the right.

At first I see some chucklehead prancing around in a Pennywise clown suit. He's holding a red balloon and sporting the archetypal Tim Curry style instead of the newer, grislier Bill Skarsgard edition. I'm hoping I don't hear a "Beep beep, Denny!" and sigh with relief to see the horror cosplayer swerve away to mug it up with a wandering Jason Voorhees in his midst. As expected, a crowd forms in a hurry, the clicks of their cell cameras probing into the pervading hum.

"Mr. Crowley," the voice says, and I try not to sing in the key of Ozzy Osbourne, since so many people have done it for me much of my life.

I see the rainbow wrist bracelet before the rest of him. Following it is an extended hand.

"My name's Randy Marcello, President and CEO of new acquisitions for Brand X Comics."

I don't see his hand pumping mine, but I feel it and the gloom which had snuck upon me after finding mine and Stefan's work discarded like a snubbed commodity start to lift away.

"I had a chance to take a break and read your book," Randy says in a far more enthusiastic manner than our first encounter. It only seemed like moments ago. "I like what you're doing. Stefan's art reminds me of Fiona Staples and she's a rock star. Don't change a thing, except maybe some more inclusivity. Diversity is key to keeping this medium alive, Denny. You have to evolve with the changing demographics. Nobody could've predicted how the landscape would change for minorities with Black Panther, Shang-Chi and Luke Cage, or for the gay community with our own Green Lantern, Kyle Radner. You have a broad scope to this story, so it should be easy to introduce a wide range of characters. What you need is a mentor and some backing. Brand X Comics can provide that if you're interested in a joint venture?"

I don't know what say to Randy Marcello. I'm shocked but I'm overjoyed. I can't wait to call, not text, Stefan. I can't be corny and snap off some expected insider trope like "Excelsior!" or "Make mine Brand

X!" nor "In brightest day or blackest night, no evil shape my sight." What used to be covert language amongst comic geeks has now become part of the standard lexicon, ever since San Diego made these cons the standard platform.

Thank you does the trick.

The End.

Afterword

Stress gets the best of many of us.

You see it everywhere, even in the most outwardly complacent of people. We're all dealing with something on some level, whether your trade is in law enforcement or the medical profession or you're on the front lines in the face of war. Even a barista at Starbucks has a lion's share of stories from the trenches. Internal collapse from stress can come through a high-pressure job, physical pain, parenthood, shaky finances, an ailing loved one, rejection of a life's work, the feeling of being unloved, or even loved in such an extreme way it feels submissive. On another angle, stress can be the result of a failed relationship. COVID, the ultimate stress plunging a proverbial crowbar into our nation, our entire *world*, prying it apart at the seams.

It's that pervading internal collapse which I was most interested in conveying with my stories for *Coming of Rage*. I wasn't concerned so much with the violence which can and often does manifest in the face of trauma. I was more interested in the will to survive, to skirt the edge with integrity when fear and doubt tests your mettle, using Allison's plight in "Watching Me Fall," for example. How cliché it would be to make her a brutalizing *I Spit On Your Grave*-type retaliator, which you can leave to Meir Zarchi. To usher revenge in a more productive, career-crippling sequence of events without resorting to killing? Such nobler retribution summons far more courage. As Allison's creator, I want to hug the heck out of her.

It's about staying calm under pressure like Mike in "In Search of Dave the Wave," based on an actual guy who *did* noodle a calling card wave symbol all over the Maryland eastern shore back in the late 1980s. I always wondered what happened to him, though many of us had a suspicion who he was. My graduating class believed "Dave" was one of us, and I'm sure other regional schools claimed the legend as well. For my purposes in this story, Dave is an uber-paranoid, fiddle-fixated dropout of society finding a new life (on the teeter of being undone) as manager of an ocean resort souvenir shop.

Sidebar, when I wrote the first draft of "In Search of Wave the Wave," Russia had not yet invaded Ukraine in 2022. Ocean City, Maryland has, in recent years, already received an influx of hard-working Ukrainian immigrants along the boardwalk. Good people, many of them. Katya is an actual person whom I met and talked to on the boardwalk, her modeling aspirations very much her mojo. The real Katya being half my age, I felt like a dad who would readily put her on a bus, plane, or train with five grand if I had it to spare. Katya's exuberance won me over and she landed in my story to give Dave the Wave a sense of gravity before he's confronted by two off-duty detectives with a long-running curiosity to satisfy more than a bust. Katya, I hope you made it to Manhattan, kid.

Despite the fangs-baring title of this collection, *Coming of Rage* is about doing the right thing, whether it's pushing off an indecent proposal in "Chasing the Moon" or standing up to injustice no matter your skin color, as in "B.L.M." I live on the outskirts of Baltimore, which has made national news the past decade, less for its honored tradition of competitive sports and more for the inner-city violence sparked by the Freddie Gray case and the Black Lives Matter movement.

I watched the often-bipolar views of CNN and Fox News while I wrote "B.L.M." What resonated with me more was seeing men and women, straight and gay, a melting pot of races, marching down the streets, all in arms. At the same time, I kept my ear open to the public and heard dissent from the black community positing whether white people had any real reason to be involved. I heard someone say in counterpoint, "Who cares when it's for doing what's right?" Thus, my story of Marcus and Sam, two aging college buddies of differing races on the protest line, came to life. Things had to get real.

Of all the tales in *Coming of Rage,* the title story is a purge. This was a time of difficulty from age 11 through 12, a time when kids should still be enjoying the waning tatters of innocence but can be crassly thrust into an adult situation, such as happened here. I filled "Coming of Rage" with a dissipating purity on purpose, since it happened in the exact way I wrote it. Consider it a personal prequel to taking matters into my own hands when the abuse from my middle school peers turned me into the most fearsome version of myself I've ever known.

Both "Dad's Notebook" and "Watching Me Fall" were first 300-plus page novels I'd written and shelved. "Dad's Notebook" was penned a year before my own father passed away. My father and I had wonderful moments together over the years, but also a lot of terrible ones. This story was built through an inner reconciliation of the bad, for which I forgave my dad the day before he died. I know he is proud of me instead of the opposite for what I came up with here. As a closet romantic, he was as fond of the gushy "Scott Secrets" and "Kate Confidentials" as I was.

Prior to writing these stories, I'd spent 16 years as a music and film journalist. I'd been writing for many magazines and websites covering metal, punk, electronic and Goth music, plus horror and indie films. It was the time of my life before re-meeting my fiancée, TJ. Before that, I'd written hockey analysis for an NHL site, I'd done beat reporting and photography for local newspapers, and I wrote serialized superhero fiction stories in the hopes of working my way into the comics' scene. It's a dream I still have, writing for the "funny books," as you may infer with the story, "Comic Con," from this collection. For the record, the real Stefan is none other than my collaborative artist partner from Kiel, Germany, Dom Valecillo.

You can see shades of my experiences in the music industry in this book, especially through "Chasing the Moon," where I recreated one of my fate-bungled assignments covering underground music. A tour manager is either a music writer's best friend or nemesis. There is seldom any middle ground. Yes, Atlas the rat was real, and he greeted me on my way out of many a show covered at The Ottobar in Baltimore.

Naturally, a de facto underlying theme to the stories making the final cut of *Coming of Rage* is music. Any memorable movie is done further justice by the imprint of a powerful score or a binding soundtrack of tunes, whether you're talking John Williams, Hans Zimmer, Jerry Goldsmith, Ennio Morricone, Isaac Hayes, Ryuichi Sakamoto or the *Guardians of the Galaxy* and *Fast Times at Ridgemont High* soundtracks. One reason *Mad Max: Fury Road* became such an instant classic was due to Junkie XL's cataclysmic score; it was so damn *epic.* Submerging into soundtracks is an integral part of my creative process.

Each story had to bear some reflection of music, the finest gift we can share with each other as humans. Music has the power to soothe, to inspire, to build memories with friends and to save our souls before stress sparks that internal collapse I mentioned. I have cultivated a disparate taste for nearly all the genres music has to offer, so long as there's honesty to what's being presented. Music has always gotten me through both the best and toughest of times and I expect it always will.

For being my best friend and restoring my drive to write, I thank and love you, TJ. Providence kept aligning our paths on and off since 1999, but here we are now, just the two of us, as Grover Washington, Jr. and Bill Withers would swoon. Call me a sap, I don't care. We can make it if we try.

To my boyo, I'm *so* proud of you, dude. I can't say enough how much I appreciate your maturity to give me the space and time I needed toward completing this manuscript. Getting up in the dark to polish stories only gets you so far. Adopting you is what your mother and I got right, never forget it. *Coming of Rage* and my future works are written for you as much as myself.

Thank you to my new friend and lexis conspirator, Tara Caribou, for taking on *Coming of Rage* with an objective eye and an exciting prospectus to launch this book through Raw Earth Ink. A coast-to-coast exchange of state magnets between Maryland and Alaska is about the coolest way to open a business venture as I can think of.

Thanks to my beta readers, TJ, Mom, Jo, Suze and others who saw the original ugly first drafts of these stories and had the veracity to call me out when things didn't work. Mom, you've been there my entire journey as writer, taking in the good with the abysmal and pumping me up in both cases. The red pen notes and your smiley doodles when I've "nailed it," who could ask for better support? Ditto for Pop, my "main man," who'll tell anyone who'd listen how I interviewed Dee Snider of Twisted Sister, then worked for him in a stint at *House of Hair Online.*

I can never repay the debt of kindness shown me by my high school Creative Writing teacher, Paul Day, who made me believe in myself in 1987 and 1988. Both he and my Expository Writing teacher at North Carroll High, Steve Hollands, invested so much in me as to make me read my assignments before their classes. It elevated my craft and endeared me to my peers. Mr. Day, it was an honor to read for you at one of my open mike headliner events later in life.

Thanks to the professors, advisors, and staff of *Spectrum,* for giving me my first music column and promotion to Assistant Editor. I don't say it as much as I should; you all challenged me and opened my future path. Professor Weber, I will always consider you as much of a colleague as a teacher.

Props to Elizabeth Kracht, literary agent and friend, for reading my work and offering me critique and advice in getting to where I am at this point. For all writers, regardless of your level of experience, I recommend Liz's invaluable writing manual, *The Author's Checklist.* It helped me put the final shine to these stories, a few nearly left for dead.

My love goes to my entire family and friends who always cheer me on. Paulette and Mark, that includes you, being there since I came out of the womb. It thrills me to have something tangible to show you for all the rallying you've given me.

I miss my Dreamers open mic crew in Frederick, Maryland, and our eternal battles to be heard against the hissing espresso machines along with those jeering rednecks and frat boys. The glorious times we had downing pints and creating art on-the-spot at Brewer's Alley on Friday nights after open mic will always hold a special place in my heart.

Finally, thank you to my grandfather, Thomas Knepp. You made the call at the kitchen table back in 1983, telling me I was destined to become a writer. It sounded like ballyhoo to me then. Today, it's my ultimate joy to prove you right.

~Ray Van Horn, Jr.

About the Author

Ray Van Horn, Jr. is a veteran journalist and author. He spent 16 years covering music and film for outlets such as *Blabbermouth*, *AMP*, *Pit*, *Dee Snider's House of Hair*, *Music Dish*, *DVD Review*, Horror News.net, Fangoria Musick, *Metal Maniacs*, *Noisecreep*,

Unrestrained, *Impose*, *Caustic Truths*, *Pitriff* and many others. Ray contributed essays to Neil Daniels' music biographies on Iron Maiden and ZZ Top. Ray's blog, "The Metal Minute" won *Metal Hammer* magazine's "Best Personal Blog" award.

Ray wrote NHL game analysis for *The Hockey Nut* and other sports articles for *Kid Shtick*. He was a beat reporter and photographer for *The Emmitsburg Dispatch* and *The Northern News*. He was the host of the forum "Comic Books" at *ReadWave*. Ray wrote serialized superhero fiction for *Cyber Age Adventures* and his fiction has also appeared at Akashic Books, *Atomic Flyswatter*, *The Rubbertop Review*, *Story Bytes* and *New Noise*, plus the anthologies "Axes of Evil" and "Axes of Evil II." He was the 1999 winner of *Quantum Muse's* fiction contest.

Ray lives with his fiancée and fellow author, TJ Perkins, in their native state of Maryland.

Made in the USA
Middletown, DE
29 September 2024

61649373R00109